the
Buccaneers

By the same author

The Wreckers

The Smugglers

Lord of the Nutcracker Men

Other titles you will enjoy

Allies of the Night: Darren Shan

The Secret Life of Sally Tomato: Jean Ure

Futuretrack 5: Robert Westall

Ella Enchanted: Gail Carson Levine

A Tale of Time City: Diana Wynne Jones

The Fatal Strand: Robin Jarvis

The Owl Service: Alan Garner

Feather Boy: Nicky Singer

Sabriel: Garth Nix

The Weathermonger: Peter Dickinson

the Buccaneers

IAIN LAWRENCE

An imprint of HarperCollins*Publishers*

First published in the USA by Bantam Doubleday Dell 1998
First published in Great Britain by Collins 2003

1 3 5 7 9 10 8 6 4 2

Collins is an imprint of HarperCollins*Publishers* Ltd,
77-85 Fulham Palace Road, Hammersmith, London W6 8JB

The HarperCollins website address is www.harpercollins.co.uk

Text copyright © 1998 Iain Lawrence
Map by Virginia Norey

The author asserts the moral right to be identified
as the author of the work.

ISBN 0 00 713556 4

Printed and bound in Great Britain by
Clays Ltd. St Ives plc

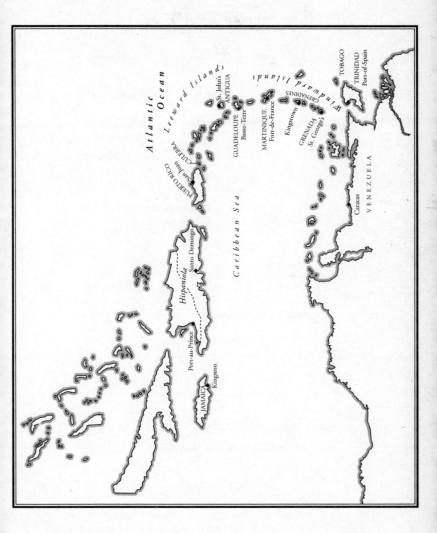

for Bruce and Lonnie,

who came sailing every day

and survived both a grounding

and a capsizing

Chapter 1

The Lifeboat

I was steering the *Dragon* when the lifeboat came into view.

It appeared ahead, a tattered sail on a sea that blazed with the evening sun. Its canvas bleached to white, its hull bearded with weeds, it looked as ancient as Moses. But it drove into the teeth of the trade winds, beating towards a land so distant that there might have been no land at all.

I felt a shiver to see such a tiny craft in such an endless waste of sea and sky. We were twenty-one days out of England, a thousand miles from any shore. But even our schooner — a little world for the eight of us aboard — seemed almost too small for the ocean.

"Sail!" I shouted, and turned the wheel. "Sail ho!"

The *Dragon* leaned under her press of canvas. With a boom and a shudder she swallowed a wave in the huge carved mouth of her figurehead. Men stirred from the deck, rising to tend the sails, and the sounds of stomping feet and squealing rope brought Captain Butterfield up from below.

The sun glinted through his greying hair and onto the pink of his scalp as he stooped through the companionway. "What's the matter, John?" he asked.

"A boat, sir." I pointed forward.

He'd brought his spyglass, and he aimed it at the distant lifeboat.

"How many people?" I asked.

He took a moment to answer. "None," he said.

"That's impossible," I told him.

He lowered the glass, wiped his eye, and looked again. The long lens stayed perfectly still as his arms and his knees bent with the roll of the ship. Then he brought it down and shook his head. "Look for yourself."

He traded the glass for the wheel, and it was all I could do to keep that glass aimed at the lifeboat. But I had to agree: there seemed to be no one aboard.

"Can we fire a gun?" I asked.

"Good thinking, John." He shouted for the gunner. "Mr Abbey! A signal, please."

For the first time in our voyage, I was glad we had our four little guns and the little man who worked them, as strange as he was. He stripped the crisp tarpaulin jacket from the nearest cannon, and had it ready to fire so quickly that I realised only then that he'd kept it loaded all the way from London.

A cloud of smoke barked from the gun. The *Dragon* shook from stem to stern, and the lifeboat flew from the circle of sea in my spyglass. Then I found it again, and there was a man staring at me, peering past the edge of the sail. He had been sitting to leeward, with that tattered rag of a sail as a shelter from the spray and sun.

"There, he's seen us," I shouted.

"And look!" cried Captain Butterfield. "Good heavens, he's turning away."

It was true. The man had put up the helm of his little boat and it now spun towards the south. As we watched, he eased the sheets and ducked his head as the sail billowed out above him. Then off he went, fleeing as fast as he could from the only bit of help that he had in all the world.

"Confound him," said Butterfield. "Is he mad?"

I thought he must have been. I saw his head looking back, turning on shoulders as broad as a bull's. Then, just as quickly, he put his helm over again, and came racing towards us.

"Heave to!" shouted Butterfield. "Best we let the devil come to us."

We turned the *Dragon* into the wind and lashed her wheel. She lay almost dead in the water, scudding sideways as the swells rolled underneath her. The captain and I — like every man aboard — stood by the rail and watched that lifeboat crawl up to weather.

Its paint long gone, its seams plugged by scraps of cloth, it looked like a feast for the sea worms. Tangles of weeds trailed in its wake; water slopped in its bilge. But the man who sailed it was bronzed and strong, as though he'd set out just the day before to sail across an ocean. An enormous sea chest of polished wood was jammed between the thwarts.

He brought his boat alongside, cast off his sheet, and dropped the tiller. Then he hoisted that great box onto his shoulder and climbed up to the deck of the *Dragon*.

"Help him below," said Butterfield. "Give him a meal and a hammock."

"Aye, sir," I said.

The men scattered as I went forward, the hands to the sails, Abbey to his gun. Only the stranger was left, sitting astride his chest and looking very much at home. His hair was tarred in a pigtail, and though his skin was deeply tanned, his eyes were a very clear blue.

"Where have you come from?" I asked.

"From the sea," he said. And that was all. He came to his feet, towering above me, and glanced up at the topsail, aft to the stern — everywhere but down at his boat, which wallowed in the swells as we left it behind.

I bent to take the man's sea chest, the finest one I'd ever seen. The rope beckets — the handles — were so elaborately knotted that months of work must have passed in their making. The wood glowed with its warm finish of oil. But I grunted at the weight of it. Though stronger than most boys of seventeen, I couldn't hope to lift that enormous box.

The stranger laughed and put it up to his shoulder again. The sound that came from inside it — a rumbling and a clinking — made me think that coins and jewels were nested there. Then he followed me down to the fo'c's'le, where I hung a hammock that he climbed into without a word of thanks.

"Would you like some food?" I asked. "Some water?"

He shook his head, his eyes already closed. In another moment he was sound asleep, swinging in the canvas as though in the great cocoon of some enormous insect.

I found a blanket and covered him, then went up to help Mr Abbey secure the gun. We stretched the tarpaulin jacket in place and lashed it down.

"There you go," said Abbey, stroking at the cloth, smoothing it over the muzzle. "You rest awhile." He had a habit of talking to his guns, and it always unnerved me. "That will keep you dry, my handsome little man-eater," he said.

He loved his guns, but I despised them. Their weight made the *Dragon* roll badly at times, and only batter through waves she would have hurdled without them. But my father had insisted on arming the *Dragon*, and whether or not to carry guns was the *only* decision he hadn't left to me. "You're going to the Indies," he'd said. "There's pirates in the Indies."

I laughed now, to think of that. What a dreadful place

the West Indies had seemed from the way Father had described them. He'd filled the waters with sharks and wood-eating worms, the sky with hurricanes that blew all the year round, and the islands with swarms of cannibals. "Yes, cannibals," he'd said. "They cook you alive, or so I've heard. They shrink your head to the size of a walnut."

But his fear of pirates had been the greatest of all, and he'd paid a fortune for the little four-pounders that sat on the deck, two to a side, with their muzzles pointing over the rail. Then, true to form, he'd found a bargain in the gunner. "Same wages as an ordinary seaman," he'd boasted. "Yet the man was serving in the navy before you were born." So great was Father's love of bargains that he overlooked Mr Abbey's years, his oddness, even the glass marble fitted in place of his left eye, in a head as round as a cannonball.

That marble gleamed crimson now, as Abbey looked up from the lashings. The sun was turning red, staining the sails. It lit a blaze right across the horizon, scattering embers of light on the sea.

"I don't like the looks of him," he said.

"Who?" I asked.

"That fellow from the lifeboat. Where did he come from and where was he bound?"

"I'm sure I don't know, Mr Abbey," I said.

"Why was he sailing into the wind?" Abbey tilted his head. "I'd ask him that, if I were you, Mr Spencer. I'd ask him why he was tacking east when he might have run to the west, where the land was closer."

"Perhaps you'll ask him yourself," I said. Then I turned away and stood at the rail.

"Count on it, Mr Spencer."

I didn't care very much for the gunner. He still sported the rags of his old naval uniform, and seemed to think that his faded gold braid and his little brass buttons made him equal to an admiral.

"I'll ask him this as well," he said, coming up to my side. "I'll ask him what he carries in that bureau of his."

I laughed. The stranger's sea chest was enormous, but not quite as big as a bureau.

"I think he's a Jonah, maybe," said Abbey.

"That's absurd," I said.

"Is it? Does he look like a man who's been adrift for weeks?"

"Perhaps he hasn't been," I said.

Abbey grunted. "But his boat has."

I wouldn't admit it to Abbey, but I'd had the same thought. The boat had grown weak, but the man was still strong.

"Try it," said Abbey. "Get into a boat and drift out there. In a matter of days, the sun turns you into a cinder. In a fortnight it makes a mummy of you, dry as old leather." He spat into the sea. "A man outlive his boat? Not a chance!"

His one good eye was closed, yet he stared straight at me with the reflected sunset glaring in his glass marble.

It was a most disturbing thing, as though he could actually see with some kind of fiery vision.

"Look in his sea chest," said Abbey. "If he's a Jonah, he'll carry his curses in there."

"That's enough!" I said.

Abbey cackled. He turned his head and looked down at the sea. The water seethed below us, and the *Dragon* churned on towards the west. She rushed down a wave, rose on the face of the next. The sun flared once more and disappeared. And Mr Abbey gasped.

He reached out and clutched my arm. "Did you see that?" he cried.

"What?" I asked.

"Right there!" he shouted. "You must have seen it." He stretched over the rail, staring straight down at the sea, then aft along the hull. He squeezed shivers of pain into my arm. "Tell me you did."

"See what?" I asked again.

"A coffin," he cried. "It looked like a coffin all nailed together, the lid swinging open." He stared at me with utter horror. "Tell me you saw it."

I tried to shake him off, but his fingers held me like talons. "I saw no such thing," I said.

"Then I'm doomed!" He let me go and slumped at the rail. "I'm finished. We all are, maybe."

"No one's doomed," said I.

His glass eye burned. "Oh, we are, young Mr Spencer. There's a Jonah come aboard."

Chapter 2

The Stranger's Tale

It was near the end of my watch — my turn at the wheel — when the captain came up from below, still in his nightclothes. He wore a purple robe that fluttered and billowed around him, baring legs as knobby and white as those of a poorly built table.

He stood behind me at the wheel. "Should we reef?" he asked. "Should we strike the topsail? Are we driving her too hard?"

"Oh, she can carry her sails," I said.

He laughed, delighted, and clapped his hand upon my shoulder. "Fancy this," he said. "Did you ever think we would play our game on a schooner's deck?"

"No, sir," said I.

The wind pulled at his robe and pushed at his nightshirt, and he took his hand away to draw his sash more tightly. "When your watch is over, fetch that stranger and bring him down below," he said. "I would like to hear his tale."

I nodded. "Yes, sir. So would I. And Mr Abbey, too."

"Abbey?"

"Yes," I said. "He told me the man's a Jonah. He saw a coffin in the sea, and now he thinks we're doomed."

Butterfield snorted. "Doomed to listen to rubbish."

"He was quite distraught," I said.

"Well, can't say I'm surprised. Gunners are mad, you know. The whole lot of them." Butterfield snatched at his robe as it flapped open again. "I think all the noise — of their cannons and their infernal banging about — must knock something loose in their skulls."

"Yes, sir," I said.

"Now let her have her head." He was already going below. "I'm afraid we'll drive her under."

I turned the wheel, smiling at the memories he'd raised of my childhood, of the hours we'd spent crouched on the floor, pushing my little wooden boats across a carpet bunched into monstrous waves. He was my father's closest friend, Uncle Stanley to me, though we weren't related by blood. He would come to the house, in those days, straight from the sea, smelling of salt and wind. "Should we reef?" I would ask. "Are we driving her too hard?" And Uncle Stanley would say, "Oh, she can carry her sails." I'd thought him absolutely fearless; it never occurred to me that he might have only wished to fetch the edge of the carpet as soon as he could, and end our game more quickly.

I nudged the wheel and sent the *Dragon* back on her wilder course. She flew along towards fading stars as the sun came up behind her. Then poor Dana Mudge emerged from the fo'c's'le and patrolled once around the deck, as he did every day at dawn. Here and there — between the guns, against the fo'c's'le break — he stooped and straightened, then waddled to the rail. It was a ritual for him to collect the flying fish that had come aboard during the night and return them to the sea.

As always, he made a report when he came to take the wheel. "Ten of the brutes this morning," he said.

"Very good," I told him.

Then he blinked and squinted, and put his hands on the spokes. He was the son of a farmer, with a ploughman's strength. But Mudge always stood to the helm like a man to a battle, wrestling the *Dragon* through the waves as though he hoped to knock her flat as soon as he could.

I went forward to wake the stranger, but found him instead at the foot of the foremast. He had his clasp knife out, and was whittling at a piece of wood. "The captain would like to see you," I said.

We went below, to a cabin lit only by the skylight. The broad windows across the stern were covered with heavy curtains, which Butterfield had fixed in place the day we'd left the land behind and hadn't opened since. He sat at his table, before a chart of the North Atlantic, under a lamp that swung wildly on its hook. His head tilted back as he took in all of the stranger's height. "What's your name?" he asked.

"Horn," said the stranger. He stepped under the skylight, the only place where he could stand erect. There, with his shoulders above the deck beams, the lamp swinging at the height of his elbows, he seemed as massive as a giant.

The *Dragon* staggered along, though the seas weren't big at all. A wooden box with Butterfield's pipe and tobacco slid down the length of the table. He watched it, then looked at me. "Mudge?" he asked.

I nodded.

"Confound him." He shook his head, then smiled at Horn. "Well, it's fortunate we found you."

"Why?" asked Horn.

"Well, come on, man," said Butterfield, perplexed. "I'm not asking you to thank me, but you were lost. A thousand miles from land."

"A little more than that, I think," said Horn. "But I wasn't lost at all. I was making for the Ivory Coast."

Butterfield looked down at his chart. He frowned at what he saw. "Do you have a sextant?"

"No."

"A log? A compass?"

Horn shook his head.

"Do you have charts?"

"No," said Horn. "But I know where I was going. I know where I started from."

"And where was that?" asked Butterfield.

Horn named a position in degrees and minutes. The captain touched his chart, his finger running west across it, nearly to the Indies. He said. "You could have fetched the Indies in a week."

"Yes, more or less," said Horn.

I frowned. "Then why sail east?"

Horn looked at me with a quick turn of his head, a gesture like a hawk's. "I wanted to go to Africa," he said.

"But why?" His eyes never blinked, and I found it easier to stare at the chart than at them.

"Well," he said. "I took a fancy to see the Ivory Coast."

Butterfield rubbed his forehead. The tobacco box hurtled down the table and thumped against his elbow. I steadied myself, and Butterfield clutched his chair. Only Horn stood easily, so straight that he might have been nailed to the deck.

"Blast that Mudge," said Butterfield. Then, to Horn, "What ship are you from?"

"Does it matter?" asked Horn.

"It matters to me," said the captain. "Look, this isn't a court of inquiry, man. We only ask what brings you here."

"Very well." Horn stared fixedly ahead. "There was a packet bound for England. The *Meridian Passage.*"

"What happened to her?"

"I believe she perished."

Butterfield's eyebrows arched. "You *believe* she perished?"

"It's safe to say she did," said Horn.

"When was that?" asked the captain.

"Twenty-six days ago."

My jaw dropped open. We'd still been tied to our London dock twenty-six days ago. In all the gales we'd weathered, in all the sunsets and the dawns we'd seen, Horn had been sailing east in his little boat. It was a feat I could never do myself, nor ever *want* to do.

"What did you eat?" I asked.

"The sea is full of fish," said Horn. "And the fish are full of water, so don't ask me what I drank. I squeezed them like lemons."

"Amazing." Captain Butterfield shook his head. "No matter what you say, this is fortunate indeed. For me, if not for you."

"Why is that?" asked Horn.

"I'll sign you aboard, of course." The *Dragon* tipped; the tobacco box clouted the captain's wrist. He picked it up and pitched it onto his bunk. "You can work the ship through the islands and home to England."

Horn nodded. "As you wish. I suppose there's little choice."

The captain brought out his log, and a quill that he dipped in ink. He offered them to Horn, who bent almost double to reach the table. The book slid away; Butterfield pushed it back. Horn took the pen and made his mark, an elegant little albatross that he sketched with three quick strokes.

Then the captain dismissed him. "I imagine you could sleep for days," he said.

"No," said Horn. "I've had my watch below, and I'd rather stand for a while."

"Then you can stand a trick at the wheel."

Horn touched his forehead — a funny little quick salute. He ducked under the beams and went out through the door.

As it latched behind him, Captain Butterfield said to me, "It's a rather strange story, John."

"Yes, sir," I said. "But I think it's true."

"So why is he so mysterious?"

I couldn't answer that. The captain's chair tipped sideways as the *Dragon* rolled. The hanging lamp jangled against its lanyard, and a locker flew open, its contents tumbling out. I tightened my shoulders, waiting for a crash of water above me. But it never came; Mudge could steer in a calm and make it feel like a gale.

Butterfield rolled his eyes at the skylight. He glanced at the rubble in the corner, then back at his chart. With his finger, he drew Horn's passage across the ocean. "Against the wind," he said. "Why?"

For pleasure, I thought. From a fancy, just as he'd said. But I didn't tell Butterfield that, for I realised then that the lamp was no longer moving, that the curtains were hanging as straight as boards at the windows. And I looked up through the skylight to see that Horn had taken the wheel.

Feet apart, hands on the spokes, he worked the helm so easily that it seemed the ship worked *him*, that the movements of her rudder came up through the wheel to drive his arms like cranks and cams. Handsome as a god, perfect in every way, he was *born* to steer a ship.

Butterfield got up and started putting in order what Mudge's clumsy steering had thrown into disarray. It amused me to think how many times he must have done that in all the years they'd sailed together in the ships my father owned. He hung his double-barrelled flintlock pistol back on its peg and returned his Bible to its place. I smiled when he plucked his socks from the locker's upper shelf and told me that he'd left them on a lower one. And when he cried out, "Oh, my poor sextant," I laughed.

"You find it funny?" he asked, whirling on me. "I'm surprised at you, John."

"I'm sorry," I said.

"He's bent the arm, I think. He's given it a good whack, at any rate." Butterfield cradled the sextant like an injured child. "Don't you see what this means?"

"Yes, sir," I said, chagrined. I only dimly understood the process that let him aim the thing at the sun or the stars and determine our position anywhere on earth. Yet

I saw quite clearly that a damaged instrument was no good at all. If we couldn't trust it, we were lost in every way there was.

"If I didn't know better," said Butterfield, "I'd say there *is* a Jonah with us now."

Chapter 3

A Jonah's Job

Horn made a place for himself in the crew, fitting in with the men like a stray dog who'd found a home. He went at every task with a will, with the strength of three men. And he was always at the wheel when the sun went down, for he loved to steer us from the day to the night, towards the first of the stars that we saw.

The spot at the foot of the foremast became his, and his alone. There he sat by day and by night, working away with his knife and his bits of wood, as though set to a lonely task of the most pressing importance. But whenever a hand was needed, Horn was the first on his feet.

Not one of the crew was really his friend, but only Mr

Abbey hated him. The gunner whispered rumours through the ship that it was a Jonah's job Horn was doing at the foot of the mast. He told stories of the enormous sea chest and the contents that shifted sometimes — when the *Dragon* rolled — with a sound that carried to the deck.

I felt almost sorry for Abbey. The *Dragon* raced along in the sunshine and the spray, but the gunner lived in a gloom cast by his vision of a coffin. He spent hours standing at the rail, either staring at the sea or glaring daggers at Horn.

Then there came an afternoon when we'd been at sea for thirty days or so. I passed the helm to Horn, and for once he started to talk about idle things in a way that any shipmate might, but in a way he'd never done himself.

"Have you ever been to the Indies, Mr Spencer?" he asked.

"No," I said.

"But you've been to sea." He held the wheel lightly, and I felt the *Dragon* surge along. "It's written all over you, Mr Spencer. She's in your blood, the sea."

This was the highest praise of all, coming from Horn. "I've been to the Mediterranean," I said. "And once across the Channel, that's all."

"It's more than many," he said. "And farther than most. Why, I've seen men cross puddles in the street and look back to see what a voyage they've made."

I grinned at the thought of that. But I didn't tell him

that my first time at sea had ended in a wreck on the Tombstones, nor that my second had nearly led to the loss of a second ship — the *Dragon* herself.

"Well, you're lucky, Mr Spencer," said Horn. "You've got a lively ship, and a pleasant captain, too. He seems kindly."

"He is," I said.

"Have you known him long?"

"All my life," said I. "When I was a boy, I—"

"Why, you're still a boy," said Horn.

"When I was a *child*, then, I called him Uncle Stanley."

"Did you?" Horn smiled, his blue eyes as bright as the sea.

"He's not my real uncle," I said. "He was a partner in my father's business. But he didn't care for the office and the books, so he went to sail the ships instead." It pleased me that Horn wanted me there, where he always stood alone. "When I was a *child*, I wished that he were my father, or that my father were more like him."

"And that's how you come to be sailing on this ship?"

"It's how *he* comes to be with *me*," I said. "My father owns the *Dragon*. I chose the captain, and together we chose the crew. They've all been hands on my father's ships."

"Except the gunner."

"Yes," I said. "Except for him."

The wheel turned and his arms moved, and I thought that if a ship could love, the *Dragon* loved Horn. She fairly flew with him at the helm.

"He's scared of the sea," said Horn.

"Mr Abbey?" I asked.

"Your captain."

"He is not," I said.

"He keeps his cabin darkened, his curtains drawn."

"He's *always* been a sailor."

"A coastwise sailor," said Horn.

He was right. Stanley Butterfield had done all his sailing close to land. "But he's not afraid," I said.

"We'll see, Mr Spencer," said Horn.

He turned his face up to the sails, and it was clear that he meant to say no more. I made my way forward and sat at the bow, my favourite spot on the ship. The enormous carved dragon that once had plucked me from the sea chewed the waves in wooden teeth, and spat out foam and spray.

I loved the fury of it, the smash of water breaking in the open mouth. The secret hatch in that dragon's throat was sealed for ever now, the compartment behind it reached only from inside the hull. That space, a relic from the *Dragon*'s smuggling past, was so dark and cramped that we called it the Cave. But it still echoed all the thunder of the sea and gave a voice to the *Dragon*, a deep and constant roar. I settled there at the bow, to watch and listen, and the last person I wanted beside me was Roland Abbey. But he sat at my side. "You were talking to Horn," he said.

"What of it?" I asked.

"Oh, it's nothing to me," said the gunner. "Myself, I'd rather talk to the fish. I'd get more answers from them."

"You don't like him," I said.

"I don't trust him," said Abbey. "Do you know what he's called in the fo'c's'le?"

"No," I said.

"Spinner. He'll spin you a fine little yarn any moment you please." Abbey bared his teeth in something less than a smile. "He spins lies into truth, that Horn. He weaves whole pictures from lies, until you'd swear what you see is the truth."

"What lies has he told?" I asked.

"What truths has he told?" countered Abbey.

The sea frothed towards our feet as the *Dragon* met a wave. The great carved head disappeared, then rose again in a churn of froth.

"Did he tell you why he turned away when he saw us?" asked Abbey. "Eh, Mr Spencer? Did he tell you that? Or how he fled from a packet in a boat that was built by the navy? Or who it was that took a lash to his back?"

"I didn't know that anyone did," I said. I hadn't seen the man without a shirt.

"If he says it was the cat, he's lying." The sun gleamed in Abbey's glass eye. "The cat-o'-nine-tails doesn't do a thing like that to a man."

"A thing like what?" I asked.

"Butchery." He spat the word. "It's something Henry Morgan might have done. Or Captain Kidd, to while away a Sunday."

"The buccaneers?" I said.

"Aye. It's their sort of work."

"But they're dead."

Abbey cocked his head. "Are they?" he asked mysteriously.

"Well, *aren't* they?" I snapped.

He looked at me with his blind eye open, his good one closed, and I didn't know if he meant to squint at me or wink. "It's not so long ago that Kidd went to the gallows. Why, the last of his shipmates died not six months ago."

"He must have been more than a hundred years old," I said.

"Aye, he looked it, all right," said Abbey. "He died hard, ranting away about blood and bones and buried treasure. Died at low water, the old parrot he had squawking like a dervish, a parade of fools come to learn the secret of Captain Kidd's treasure."

"Where is it?"

"In the Indies, of course."

I felt a twinge of excitement, a tingling in my breast. From the tales I had read of the buccaneers I imagined the islands were riddled with treasure pits. "Where in the Indies?" I asked.

"Maybe Spinner can tell you."

I turned towards the wheel, leaning sideways to see round the masts. The sails cast big, square shadows on the deck, but a shaft of sunlight fell on Horn where he stood on the quarterdeck, more like a god than ever.

"Look at him," said Abbey. "Thinking he's better than anyone else. Telling me how to care for my guns."

"Ah," I said softly. I understood then why the man disliked Horn so much. Nothing would anger the gunner more than being told how to look after his cannons.

"He told me to load them with chain," said Abbey. "Chain! When it's roundshot that you want against pirates."

His fierceness alarmed me. "What makes you think we'll be fighting pirates?"

"Well, there's always a chance," he said, and looked down at the sea. "My guns are getting hungry."

I nearly laughed at the tone of his voice. It was all he wanted, I could see — to get a crack at a pirate ship, to relive a bit of the glory from his years long past. I remembered the day he'd come aboard, wrapped in his tattered cloak, a beggar boy at his heels to carry his canvas duffel. "Who's the old blind man?" I'd asked my father, and he'd laughed an embarrassed sort of laugh. "Why, that's your gunner," he'd said.

I looked at Abbey now, and had to squint against the glare in his glass eye. "*Are* there still pirates?" I asked.

"Picaroons!" he said, using an ancient word as though that alone diminished them. "It's all that's left, and not many of them. Keep clear of Hispaniola, stay away from Cuba and New Orleans, and you'd find a kangaroo before you'd see a picaroon."

It was hard to tell if he saw this scarcity of pirates as a

pleasure or a disappointment. But then his rage at Horn bubbled again to the surface. "Chain!" he said. "If you're close enough for *that*, the battle's lost."

He knocked his fist on the deck and cursed. "It will be a grand day when we fetch Jamaica and Horn goes ashore for good."

"He's not going ashore," I said.

The gunner looked up. "You didn't sign him aboard, did you?"

"Yes," said I. "He made his mark, an albatross."

"The *man's* an albatross." Abbey grunted. "Never touches land. Watches everything and seldom speaks. Listen, Mr Spencer: no good has ever come from an albatross. No good at all. And ill befall the one who harms him."

Chapter 4

A Death Ship

The stories of Horn and his sea chest flew round and round the ship like birds through a house of glass. I heard from George Betts that the box was full of pistols, and from Harry Freeman that it was shaman's bones that rattled in there. But in the end, the story that Abbey told was the one that came to be seen as the truth, though neither he nor anyone else had ever lifted the lid of that strange and wonderful chest.

"I don't *need* to see inside it," Abbey told me one day. By his own account, he was the expert on Jonahs. "I *know* what's in there."

"Then tell me," I said. And I listened to his story, then went below to tell it again to the captain.

It was just after noon on Horn's twelfth day aboard, and we sat in the shadows of the curtained cabin while Butterfield worked out his sextant sights.

"Abbey says he knows what Horn keeps in his chest," I said.

"Does he?" Butterfield was thumbing through his almanac. "And what does he say, exactly?"

"That it's full of bits of ships," I said. "That Horn travels from one to another and takes something from each."

The captain sniffed. "What a strange pastime. Why would he want to do that?"

I tried to tell him in the same words that I'd heard from Abbey. I remembered how the sun had glinted in the glass eye, and how that wizened head with its helmet of grey hair had turned up towards me. "All those pieces of wood, those bits of metal, they're his Jonah charms. He uses them in voodoo magic," I said.

The captain laughed wholeheartedly. "Jonah charms! You don't believe that rubbish, do you?"

"No, sir," I said, though in truth I had started to wonder. "But I'm afraid others might. I'm afraid Abbey will turn their heads."

Butterfield jotted numbers on a bit of paper. "What would you do about it, John?"

"We could have Horn open the chest and show us what he keeps in there."

"And lose his trust?" said Butterfield. He turned to his

reduction tables, to such long columns of numbers that I felt dizzy to see them. "No, it's best to let this run its course."

"But where will it end?"

"It will just peter out, I should think." He ran his fingers down the columns. "Our Mister Abbey's got his nose out of joint. The crew have never looked up to *him*, much to his dismay. It's no wonder he doesn't like Horn."

The captain got down to his business then, his strange mathematics. He turned his sextant angles into a real place on earth, and *that* — to me — was voodoo magic. Every day for twenty days I had listened as he'd tried to teach me. But I'd never had a head for numbers, and hadn't learned a thing. So we had both given it up as a hopeless task, and this was the first time that I'd seen him do the sights in all the time that Horn had been aboard.

Now I watched as he worked out his time and his distance, and I waited for the moment when he would take up his pencil, make a mark on the chart, and tell me, "Handy-dandy, here's where we be." Twenty times I had heard him tell me that. And at last he said it again.

But this time there was a terrible doubt in his voice. And he added, "Or it's fairly close, I hope."

I looked at the chart and saw that his crosses didn't line up. They marched in a nearly perfect line out of the Channel, south to the trades, and west across the ocean. But then they took a dogleg, a sudden bend that seemed very odd to me, and carried on with greater space between them. I counted back along the crosses, and saw that the break in the line marked the day that Mudge had sent the sextant flying from the locker.

"You don't know where we are," I said. "Do you?"

"Not exactly," he admitted. "Mudge has made a liar of the sextant." Butterfield tapped his pencil on the last of its crosses. "You see? It's telling me we're here, but I know we're not."

"Then where are we?" I asked.

He sketched a large circle around the cross. "Somewhere in here, I suppose. But it doesn't matter, really. We can only carry on and find out where we are when we get there."

I shook my head, the dizzy feeling coming back. "But why are they farther apart?"

"Why do you think?" asked Butterfield.

"The *Dragon*'s going faster now?"

"Exactly," he said.

"Then we're running with our eyes closed."

He smiled. "Yes, in a manner of speaking. But if the wind stays steady we're bound to hit the Indies, just not at the point we were aiming for."

"You'll get a new sextant in Kingston?" I asked.

The captain gaped at me. "I most certainly will not. Sextants aren't like oranges, John. You don't pick a new one from a basket." He shook his head. "I've had mine for longer than you've been alive, and I'd like to keep it, thank you very much. When I learn the error, I'll know what correction to make. There's no danger then, once we know where we are."

I was barely listening. As Butterfield spoke I'd been staring at the crosses, counting them again. And now I thought that what they really marked was Horn's first morning aboard. It seemed that he had brought a new strength to the *Dragon*, and was sending her rushing along towards a place that was known only to her. Or only to her and Horn.

"Oh, blast that Mudge!" Butterfield threw his pencil down. It landed on the chart, but moved no farther. Nothing moved: not the lamp or the curtains or the pistol on its peg. Horn was steering, and his shadow fell through the skylight and lay on the table. "Ah, Horn," said Butterfield.

"You don't think he's a Jonah, do you?" I asked.

"Of course not," said the captain. "It's a travesty to ask me that."

"Why?"

"Read your Bible, John. Jonah the prophet was trying to flee from God when the storm came up that nearly sank his ship. Yes, God made the storm and, yes, He calmed the seas when Jonah was pitched over the side. But why? To save the ship? Not on your life! To save the prophet, John. God would never let the prophet drown."

I couldn't argue with Butterfield when it came to the Bible. He knew it back to front. Yet I could see that things had changed in the days that Horn had been aboard.

Dana Mudge had become a pariah for his part in breaking the sextant. Mr Abbey was still wallowing in gloom, and the captain was beset with worries. And now the winds were blowing harder, driving the *Dragon* on her secret course.

Butterfield put away his sextant and his almanacs. I watched Horn's shadow tilt across the table, his arm moving with the wheel as the *Dragon* slithered through the waves.

"What do *you* think he carries in his chest?" I asked.

"I neither know nor care," said he. "Now that's enough of that. If there's anyone on this ship who means any harm, it's our blasted gunner for spreading this nonsense."

"Yes, sir," I said.

"It seems the only head he's turned is yours. Now go on. I have to get my socks lashed down before Mudge takes the wheel again."

I left the cabin and climbed up the companionway, two rungs at a time. At the top, I came face to face with Horn. He was looking at the sails, singing barely over his breath the song called "Heart of Oak", the tune that navy drummers beat as ships sail into battle: "*Cheer up, my lads, 'tis to glory we steer—*" Then he found me, with that quick turn of his head, and the song ended on the instant.

"You sing as well as you steer," I said.

He didn't answer. The *Dragon* leaned to a puff of wind;

her wheel turned, his arms cranked, and she steadied herself before it. He was a part of the ship; he *was* the ship, it seemed.

His eyes passed over me, his gaze running down the luff of the mainsail, past me — and through me — to the wind-swollen jibs at the bowsprit. He had no thought for anything but the passage of the ship. I stepped up to the deck, anxious to hurry past him.

"She talks, doesn't she, Mr Spencer?"

It was only an idle phrase, surely, the old idea that a ship could speak to a helmsman through the sound of her wood and rope, and tell him what trim she liked. But I thought of Turner Crowe, who'd met his death swinging from her halyards on my first voyage aboard the *Dragon*. He'd believed the schooner had a soul trapped inside her, the spirit of his son, which spoke to him at times in the creak of the *Dragon*'s planks.

"What does she say?" I asked.

"Why, what every ship says," said Horn. "Every ship and every sailor. That she'd like to run for ever where the water's deep and blue. That she's scared of the land. And if she had her fancy, she'd never see it again."

It was almost like poetry, coming from Horn. The Jonah talk seemed silly then, nothing more than the ranting of a half-mad gunner.

But not an hour later my doubts came rushing back.

It was Mudge who saw it. Horn had given up the wheel only moments before, and had gone forward to his spot at the mast. To leeward, Mr Abbey was staring aft, down our broken and weaving path through the waves. I saw Mudge stiffen and point.

"Land!" he cried. "I think I see land."

The captain groaned. "Good Lord. He'd have to be mighty farsighted for that. We've hundreds of miles to go."

But it did look like land. I peered past the sails and past the men who rushed to the bow, and I saw a tiny island with three bare trees that were tossing in the wind. It slipped behind the swells, then rose again, and I saw a line of surf at its shore. It vanished again, reappeared, and there seemed to be children swinging from the trees.

Horn stood up, but he didn't go forward with the others. He looked ahead at that strange land, then turned and looked at *me*. In the whole ship he was the only soul looking back, and Abbey didn't fail to notice.

"You'd think he'd seen it before," said the gunner.

The *Dragon* rushed along. Mudge steered us towards that land, and I saw that it wasn't land at all. It was a ship, or the hulk of a ship, her bare masts rooted in a waterlogged hull. The swells rolled over her rail and burst in white spray on her cabins. And what I'd thought were children were the corpses of her crew.

They were dead; all dead. The sun had dried them into mummies, into things that hardly looked like men. They dangled in nooses from the yards and the stays, some close to the deck and others high above it. They all swung back and forth, round and round. They made me think of shrivelled flies, of a spider's prey hanging from its web.

We sailed close along her side, and our wake — as she rolled — slurped through the ragged wounds of cannon shots. The swinging corpses seemed to turn and watch us, and the lowest ones danced on the water.

"I told you!" cried Abbey. "Look where your Jonah brought us now."

"Be quiet, man," said Butterfield. He was trembling; his lips were white.

"Didn't he steer us here?" shouted Abbey. "In all the ocean this is where he brought us, to see his Jonah's handiwork."

"Silence, I told you!" snapped Butterfield. The gunner's voice was loud enough to carry right to the bowsprit, and the crew were looking back at us now. "Take in the sails," the captain shouted down at them. "Mudge, bring us into the wind."

The men returned to their work, but Horn came aft. Walking at first, then running, he climbed to the quarterdeck with his hands in fists. Butterfield moved forward, stepping between him and Abbey.

"Cast him adrift," cried the gunner to the captain. Abbey seemed quite pleased to have Butterfield where he was. "Give him command of his Jonah's ship and let him sail wherever he pleases."

"I'm not a Jonah," said Horn.

Abbey cackled. "You tell us, Spinner."

"Sir," said Horn, the first time I'd heard him use that word. "I'm blessed, I truly am. I'm the most blessedest man that ever was."

"Oh, there's a fine yarn," cried Abbey.

"I can prove it."

"Give us another!" shouted the gunner.

"That's enough!" said Butterfield. "Mr Abbey, you will please attend to your duties."

The gunner tipped his head. "What duties?"

"Surely there's *something* you can do."

"I could sink her," said Abbey hopefully. "I could send her down where she belongs."

"Very well." The captain nodded. "Take the boat across and bring back those bodies. Get them ready for burial, then see to your guns." He turned to Horn. "Now, what proof do you have?"

"Come below and I'll show you," said Horn.

Chapter 5

Horn's Chest

I followed the captain, who followed Horn, from the quarterdeck to the bow, and down to the fo'c's'le. There the three of us stood at the foot of the ladder, in a space even darker than the captain's cabin, looking down at Horn's mysterious box.

There it sat, wedged beside the ladder, gleaming in the light from the scuttle. The beautiful beckets hung at the ends, lifting and falling with the roll of the ship, tapping at the wood. The skulls or the shaman's bones — or *whatever* was in there — seemed to answer with their own rattles and taps.

Horn reached inside his shirt. He pulled out a key that hung on a loop of sailmaker's twine. He dropped to his knees and bent over the chest, feeling along its front. Wood rasped against wood; Horn groped with the key still on his neck, and a hidden latch sprang open. He came up on his haunches and lifted the lid a fraction.

"What do they think I've got in here?" He looked up, and I was afraid to see those eyes of his, such a bright and honest blue. "Eh? What do they think is so important that it can sink ships and steer us to their wrecks like a witch's compass?" He spoke like a schoolmaster to a pair of naughty children.

I could scarcely wait to see inside the box, and his delay annoyed me. "Well, what's so important," I asked, "that you keep it under lock and key?"

"Privacy," he said simply. "Respect."

He threw the lid wide open and we leaned forward — the captain and I — and stared down at nothing but clothes. Duck trousers neatly folded, a shirt like the one he wore, a shore-going pair of shoes — all a bitter disappointment. He took them out, and underneath were bottles. A dozen or more were nested there, each covered to its shoulders in a thick woollen sock.

Butterfield laughed. I knew he was looking at me, but I didn't look back.

Horn put his hands into the box and took up one of the bottles. He held it as tenderly as the captain had held his sextant. Then he peeled back the cover. And I gasped.

There was a ship in his bottle. There was a beautiful, three-masted ship sailing on a sea painted with whitecaps.

She flew a cloud of little sails, all cut from cloth and lashed to the yards in the proper way. The courses billowed, the topsails above them, studding sails set on mere slivers of wood. There was a curl of foam at her bow, a wake at her stern, and the tiny flags reached to the very top of the bottle.

Horn pulled the others out, one by one, and I gazed at miniature brigs and men-of-war, at frigates two to a bottle. Each was perfect. All were captured in their little worlds, granted by Horn the wish he believed they wanted, to run for ever before winds that were fair.

"They were mine," said Horn. "At any rate, I sailed on them."

"They're wonderful," said Butterfield.

Horn passed a bottle to him and another to me. Mine held a brigantine that tore through a stormy sea. Warped by the glass, the ship seemed to tilt and move, the little waves to break in streaks of foam.

"It's my life in these bottles," said Horn. He began to put the others back, each in its sock, each in the chest. "If I lost one, I would lose everything that went with her, I think."

The tiny ship was rigged with shrouds and stays, with topping lifts and sheets. I marvelled as I examined her from every angle, even through the bottom of the bottle, where the glass was like a magnifier. I couldn't imagine how Horn had squeezed that model through the neck.

"That's the *Pointer Star*," he said. "My first ship." He reached up and tapped my bottle with his finger. "I took a shaving from her ribs to make the model. I took shavings from them all."

Bits of ships. So Abbey had come close to the truth, yet got it all wrong. For every real ship Horn had fashioned an offspring, a child identical to its mother.

I was touched by that. "You've made children of them all?"

"Children?" He smiled, his blue eyes glinting. "Yes, they're that," he said. "But more like orphans, really."

"What do you mean?" asked the captain.

Horn took the bottle from me. "What you see in here, it's all that's left. The *Pointer Star* lies fathoms down off the Fastnet rock."

The *Dragon* rolled and the bottles shivered. Horn's voice dropped to a whisper. "It's the same with all the others. Their mothers are gone, every one of them. Some by cannon shot, some by storms. Some just disappeared."

There was a creak of wood, a tremble of the hull, as the *Dragon* battered through a wave.

"Every one?" asked Butterfield.

"Every blessed one," said Horn, and shook his head as though bemused. "It's the strangest, damnedest thing."

I shared none of his humour. I felt icy cold to think that every ship he'd sailed upon had come to ruin. As he laid my bottle down among the others, I looked at his chest with its lid swung open, and a tingle went racing through my spine. It was a wooden coffin that Horn had built, a tomb for lost ships.

"So it's true," I said. "You *are* a Jonah."

"Not at all." He seemed surprised that I would think it. "I'm blessed, as I told you. There's no one as blessed as me."

"How?" I asked.

"Didn't you listen?" His eyes turned towards me, bright in the shadows. "The fates had it in for those ships; I don't know why. But they don't have it in for me, do they? Not a one of those ships perished while I was aboard."

I looked at the captain, and he looked at me. Then he pointed at the chest. "Is your last ship in there?"

"No," said Horn. "She'll be the next one."

It sounded ominous the way he said it. "You mean the *Meridian Passage*?" I asked.

He frowned, then shook his head. "Packets don't count. Nor lighters and wherries. I only care about the ships I work, the ones I sign aboard."

"Like the *Dragon*," I said, with a shiver.

"Aye." He fixed me in the stare of those blue eyes. "But don't worry, Mr Spencer. There's no vessel as safe as the one that has old Horn aboard." He winked, and it was like a lantern briefly shuttered. "As long as she keeps him there, you see."

Ill befall the one who harms him. I remembered Abbey's words.

"So now you know," said Horn. The lock clicked into place as he closed the lid. "And now you can tell your gunner and all the others. You can tell them there's nothing but bottles in here."

We all went up to the deck, where the crew of the wretched ship now lay in a row, wrapped in shrouds of canvas wrappings. They looked small, like children again.

Horn went off to help with the burial, the captain to fetch his Bible. I helped Abbey ready the guns and told him everything that we had seen and heard in the fo'c's'le.

"Only bottle?" he said as I finished. "They're a damn sight more than that. They're his Jonah charms, just as I told you."

Indeed, he *had* come very close to the truth. But in *his* mind Horn was malicious, while in mine and Butterfield's he was merely dogged by bad luck. And I could see that nothing would change the gunner's mind.

We held a service in the sunshine for the poor souls whose names we never knew. We sent them below, where the sea was so deep that it was measured in miles and not fathoms. On the quarterdeck, Butterfield led us through a solemn hymn. He rattled off whole verses from the Bible, word for word, without once looking down at the book in his hands. Then he said a little prayer and nodded to Mr Abbey.

"Very well. You may commence firing," he said.

It seemed odd to go straight from prayers to guns. But Roland Abbey at last seemed free of his gloom. His grey head bound in a scarlet neckerchief, he ordered us about as though the *Dragon* were a ship of the line. He did none of the shooting himself, but stood aside and shouted commands at the top of his voice.

My father, of course, had not bought the best of powder and shot. The guns sometimes fizzled, and a few of the shots soared off in curves, like errant cricket bowls. But that was no excuse for our dreadful gunnery; we didn't score a single hit until the ships drifted so close together that we might have bowled the balls across by hand.

Abbey gave us each a turn at the various tasks of loading and sponging, of pulling the lanyards that fired the guns — or all except for Horn, who was kept at the most dreadful of the chores. The huge sailor stood high on the rail, veiled in smoke when the guns went off, in swirls of steam as he rammed his sponge down a red-hot barrel.

I watched him when my turns were done. He went at the task with a will, pausing only to haul off his shirt. He twisted his key up on its string, then bent again to his work.

Abbey nudged my shoulder. "You see what I mean?" he asked. "What manner of devil did that?"

Horn's back was covered with scars. The flesh had once been torn from his spine, and the livid remains of those hideous wounds pulsed like so many veins. Now they writhed across his back as he thrust the sponge above his head, holding it up in a savage triumph. I heard a roar and realised that the men were cheering, that the mysterious ship was finished.

She went down bow first, with a great frothing of the sea, with wrenching groans in her timbers. The cheering faded away; we watched her settle in grim silence, for there was a grace and a dignity in her death. Then all that was left was a swirl of flotsam on the water and a patch of bubbles that came rushing towards us. Below the surface, the ship was still sailing, passing under our keep on her last voyage to Davy Jones. It gave me goose bumps to think of her sliding through the darkness, through such abysmal depths where the shrouded bodies of her men were probably *still* spiralling down past the fish and the whales. I saw the bubbles break against our starboard side, and felt a thump below me, a tap against our keel.

I peered down and saw something solid come rising from the sea. I clutched the rail and cried aloud. It was Abbey's coffin, I thought, or his vision of a coffin somehow come into being.

Chapter 6

Fiddler's Green

Long and narrow, wrapped in weeds, that thing like a coffin shot from the water, right before my eyes, with a burst of spray and a nearly human gasp of bubbles. It rose so high that it stood nearly on its end, then fell back and floated at the *Dragon*'s side. Then I saw that it was only a boat, a little dory with its oars still lashed neatly to the thwarts.

There was something awful about that boat, as encrusted as it was with sponges and sea growth. It seemed as though Davy Jones himself had sent it back for one more voyage to fetch another lot of seamen to his locker. But at the same time it seemed quite brave and hopeful, the only survivor of an unknown ship. And the captain said, "Haul it aboard."

For the first time Horn shirked a task. He would neither touch a line nor lay a hand to that boat; he was all for leaving it behind, for filling it with shot until it sank with the rest. But we raised it up nonetheless, and headed on to the Indies, which we sighted ten days later.

I had looked forward to that moment since the day we'd left London. I had imagined that we would greet the land — the New World — with a great celebration, that we might dance on the deck like barefooted pagans. But it was a solemn moment when the islands came into view, mere smudges on the water. Captain Butterfield stooped and touched a knee to the deck. And Horn looked at the land with despair on his face, like a man peering up at his gallows.

The islands grew larger and darker. We saw the bright green of trees, the grey of bare rock. We saw more islands beyond the first, and more after those, until they stretched in a chain in either direction. There was no obvious gap between them, no passage to take.

"Where are we?" I asked the captain.

"I'm afraid I don't know," he said. "Perhaps you'll fetch the chart."

I brought it up from below and Butterfield spread it on the quarterdeck. He knelt over it, looking now at the land and now at the chart. Mr Abbey joined him and did the same, and they looked so much like a pair of chickens pecking at the deck that I nearly laughed out loud.

"This isn't funny," snapped Butterfield, seeing my grin. "We're lost; can't you see that?"

"Yes, sir," I said.

"There's only one passage that keeps us high to windward and free of dangers. But where is it?" He waved towards the land. "Where's Antigua in all that lot?"

"Horn would know," I said.

"Spinner, aye!" cried Abbey. "He'll give us a yarn and send us on a wild-goose chase, no doubt."

"Be quiet," said Butterfield. "John's right."

So Horn, too, was brought aft. He took one look at the land, and not so much as a glance at the chart. "Turn north," he said.

"Are you sure?" asked the captain.

Horn pointed. "That's Martinique you see there, off the larboard bow."

Butterfield spread his fingers across the chart. He measured a distance of almost two hundred miles to Antigua. "We can't be off by *that* much," he said.

"Then hail that trader there," said Horn, "and ask her if I'm wrong."

"What trader?" Butterfield again squinted towards the land. Abbey stood beside him, squinting too, and I as well. Finally I saw it, white against the land, a tiny triangle scudding to the north.

"There," I said.

"Blast me," said my uncle Stanley. "I just can't see it. Still, if the boy says it's there, that's good enough for me."

Horn snorted. He wandered off as we turned to the north and closed on the trader. She was sloop rigged, slower than the *Dragon*, and we overtook her quickly, in an arc that took us up her wake. Soon we saw the helmsman, sitting lazily with his feet against the tiller. He looked towards us.

And leapt to his feet.

The little trader burst into activity, suddenly alive with tiny figures. Every sail that she could carry was hauled aloft in a madman's rig of much-patched canvas. Heeling hard, nearly driven under, she raced towards a reef where the rollers were bursting in ragged lines of white.

"Gracious!" said Butterfield, staring after her. "There's a fine welcome for us."

We carried on — to the north, as Horn had advised. We came across a second sloop, sailing south, but she turned and raced to the west. Then a third trader, coming out from the land, went beetling back again.

"Confound it!" said Butterfield. "Do they think we are lepers?"

Little Roland Abbey was beside himself. "Let me have a crack at them with the guns," he said. "I'll show them what we are."

For three days we tramped to the north, and every boat we saw fled at the sight of us. Then we found Antigua just where Horn had said, and threaded through the islands to the Caribbean Sea and its waters of blue and gold. The next morning, we saw the mountains of Jamaica, so high that clouds covered them like snow.

It was the fifty-third day of our passage when we

rounded the tip of the Palisadoes peninsula and came into Kingston Harbour. From the wheel, I saw the bay open up and the flat, bustling city appear ahead. To starboard, below the guns of Fort George, the English warships lay to their anchors off old Port Royal, packed into columns and rows like a wall of wooden bricks. We glided past them with the mainsail shaking, and a flurry of pennants rose from the ships and the naval station. Hoist after hoist went up, a furious signalling from ship to ship and fleet to shore.

"They're gossiping like a lot of fishwives," said Abbey. Many of the hoists were strange to him, but he got at least the sense of what the ships were saying. "They're wondering who we are and where we've been. It seems they think we're something of a mystery."

"At least they're not running away," said Butterfield. He stood with his hands behind his back, telling me to steer first for a mountain and then for a church when it came into view. We saw the docks and the quays; then he shouted, "Luff up!" and I turned the *Dragon* into the wind.

She stopped, then drifted back with a slattering of sails. "Let go!" called Butterfield, and down went our anchor. And there we lay, fixed again to the earth but half a world from home, in the same bay that had sheltered Blackbeard and Morgan and Kidd.

My legs ached for a run across the green slopes, my heart begged to explore a new world. But the ship came first, with her score of needs, before any man could leave her. And before *I* could hope to go, there was a cargo to unload and another to find, for a ship must earn her way. So we set to work in the heat and sounds of Kingston, and only my mind went wandering.

It was the same for all of us. Long glances were cast at the shore as we bundled the sails and coiled the halyards. My feet were on the deck, but my head was up in the mountains when the navy sent a boat to meet us. It darted across the harbour with six men at the oars and an officer steering. He was a lieutenant, but barely older than me, a Scottish boy with a flame of hair swelling like tufts beneath his hat. He hailed the deck and asked, "What ship are you?"

Butterfield answered him from the quarterdeck rail. "The *Dragon*," he said.

"From England?"

"Yes."

His voice was too boyish to reach very far. But it was the first that we had heard apart from our own, and the crew gathered closer to hear. Only Horn didn't bother with the boy. He stayed aloft on the topsail yard, fussing all by himself with a sail that was already furled.

The lieutenant looked up at our captain. "Did you see any sign of the *Prudence*?"

"I wouldn't know her," said Butterfield.

"A black schooner like yours, but with twelve guns," said the boy in his brogue. "We thought you might be her coming in, until we saw that great beastie on your bow."

Butterfield muttered under his breath, then shouted down at the boat. "What of her?"

"She's overdue in England," said the lieutenant. The rowers and the man at the tiller were all looking up. "It seems she's lost, sir."

"We saw her not," said Butterfield. "I'm sorry."

The young lieutenant touched his hat and bid his rowers to backwater. He sat at his tiller, then popped to his feet again. "Her captain's Bartholomew Grace," he said. "If you hear anything of her, will you report it to the admiral?"

"I will, sir," said Butterfield.

The boat turned and started back towards the fleet, its six oars swinging like two. We went back to our work, and soon I watched our own longboat rowing away, carrying all but myself and Abbey and Horn. The huge, bronzed sailor had no wish to step ashore, and he vanished below, into the shade of the fo'c's'le. Abbey claimed to be too old for the pleasures of Kingston; he chose to spend his day among the guns, making me think that he was really hoping for a sudden attack by picaroons. And I was left in charge, a mixed blessing to be sure.

Our cargo of wool was ferried ashore in lighters crewed by black-skinned men. The boats left full and returned the same way, packed with water and provisions. An afternoon wind brought an illusion of coolness that pleased me at first, until the wind brought a stench from a decrepit old ship anchored deep in the bay.

I helped Abbey polish his guns, but spent more time staring than polishing. I leaned on the rail and gazed at the shore, and at the ranks of warships with their yards perfectly squared. Behind them, the ruins of the ancient pirate haven writhed in waves of heat.

"If there's such a thing as ghosts, that's where you'll find them," said Abbey. "The old buccaneers stroll beneath the harbour with the fish and the worms, so they say. When it's dark, they come wading out, cloaked in dripping weeds."

He twitched. "I guess that's where I'll be soon enough, down at Davy Jones or aloft at Fiddler's Green." For a moment he stopped polishing. "Do you think there's such a place?"

"Don't talk like that," I said.

"Why not?" he asked. "My days are numbered, and I'd like to know what becomes of a man when he's gone. When you see a coffin passing by, you begin to wonder."

"You saw shadows," I said. "A trick of the light."

Abbey shook his head. He started polishing again, in places already polished. "It must be cold and dark in Davy Jones's, but they say it's warm and it never rains in Fiddler's Green."

I watched him, and I saw a tear fall from his cheek and splash on the cannon. He rubbed it away.

"Maybe you get a choice," he said. "If you like the sea, you go down to Davy Jones. And if you're like me, and you do your sailing close to land, you go up to the Green instead, where there's dancing and taverns and trees to sit under. What do you think, John?"

"I don't know," I said.

"We'll find out soon enough." He patted the gun. "Not long to wait now."

"Until what?" I asked.

"I don't know," said he. "Not exactly. But I had a dream last night. I saw a rain of iron, a flood, a pestilence, and a fire. That will be the end, I think. The fire."

I couldn't listen any more. I moved to the top of the cabin and sat by the little dory that had come from the drifting death ship. Its crust of growth had hardened, smelling strongly of the rich odour that makes landsmen think of the sea — but sailors of the shore — and I picked idly at the shrivelled sponges and weeds. Below them the dory was white-painted, with a crisp red stripe at her sheer, a once-pretty boat that I hoped to make pretty again. I covered the cabin's top with scraps of green and grey as the lighters banged against the *Dragon*'s hull in the chop of the afternoon winds. The stronger the wind blew, the worse was the smell from the rotting ship, and I longed to get to sea again. But we unloaded only half our cargo that day.

In the morning another ship arrived, as putrid and seaworn as the other. It passed in a cloud of the same dreadful stench, but went straight to the wharf, where the hatches were opened. And a sound came out of that ship, a terrible moan and a howl.

Again, I was left with Abbey and Horn, and once more the lighters scuttled back and forth. Lightened of her burden, the *Dragon* floated higher, and I stood at the stern, staring down at her outer planks, which were thick with weeds. Like a man, the ship had grown tangled beards during the passage. There was already enough grass to feed a cow, and I was thinking that she would have to be careened and scraped before we left for home, when Horn came up beside me.

"It's done," he said.

"What's done?" I asked.

From behind his back he brought out a bottle, and a sight that made my knees feel weak. Inside, a little schooner heeled to a lively breeze. Black-hulled, white-winged, the *Dragon* flew through gouged-out waves.

Chapter 7

The Slave Trader

The bottle glowed from the sun. Horn offered it to me, but I wouldn't take it. The curse of all his other ships suddenly seemed too real and too close. But neither could I look away. And the closer I studied his model, the more I saw that it wasn't right. The topsail was too big, the deck carved flush with only a small quarterdeck. The gaffs peaked higher than they ought to.

I said, "You've got it wrong."

"I don't," said Horn.

"The *Dragon* doesn't look like this," said I.

"Well, it's not the *Dragon*, then."

He sounded annoyed; I had hurt him with my words. But I felt such a strange relief that I took the bottle and told him, "It's a fine little ship."

"My last one," said Horn. "That's just as she was when I left her."

"The *Meridian Passage*?" I asked.

"No." Softly, he added, "She was a packet."

"And packets don't count," I said, repeating his earlier phrase.

"They don't." He reached for the bottle but I wouldn't give it up.

"What's her name?" I asked.

"You wouldn't know her," said Horn.

"I might."

"You wouldn't." His hands moved fast as lightning as he snatched the bottle from me. "I shouldn't have shown you this."

"Then why did you?" I asked, hurt by his tone.

"I thought we were shipmates," said he.

"We are," I cried.

"Then leave me in peace," said Horn. His arms trembled; his fist squeezed the bottle. "That's what shipmates do. They don't badger each other like this."

I couldn't understand his sudden mood. "I only asked the name of your ship."

"Good day, Mr Spencer," he said with a snarl. He turned on his heels and stalked away.

"Wait!" I shouted, but he didn't stop. I sat for a while, confused by his outburst, trying to see what I'd done to offend him. I went back to the dory and scraped at its planks as I wondered how much I knew about Horn.

Precious little, I soon saw — only that he'd set off in a lifeboat from a packet called *Meridian Passage*, and that he once had sailed on a ship that looked much like the *Dragon*. Then I thought of the young lieutenant who had asked about the ill-fated *Prudence*. "We thought you might be her," he had said. "Until we saw that great beastie on your bow."

I nodded to myself. The *Prudence* was a navy ship and it made sense that Horn had been in the navy. In the last nine months, after England and France signed their peace at Amiens, thousands of sailors had been turned ashore. Horn could have been among them, or even among the thousands of others who had stayed in the navy, for the peace had not seemed likely to last. There had been talk of another war long before the *Dragon* had departed a cold and wintry England for her voyage to the Indies.

Was it only a coincidence that the *Prudence* was reported lost just as Horn appeared in his lifeboat? His navy-built lifeboat? I felt as though I was getting close to the truth, but I had no time to think it out. Our holds were empty at last, and a man arrived just then to measure us for a new cargo.

He was blond and fat, sunburned to a red crisp on his face and his hands. He looked like a strawberry sitting in his boat. And he heaved himself up at the shrouds, gasping breaths through his nose. He called me "boy". "Who's in charge here, boy?" he asked.

"I am," I said.

"Oh?" He raised his eyebrows, and the burnt skin on his forehead wrinkled. "And who are you?"

"John Spencer," I said.

He grunted. "Are there any *men* about?"

"None who'd care to talk to you." I didn't like the man at all.

For half an hour he paced through the holds with small and awkward steps. He carried a little red notebook, and a pencil stub that he licked over and over. The wind picked up, thick with its odours, before the man climbed out again. He took a moment to catch his breath.

"Well, she's small," he said, to himself more than to me. "But she'll do, I suppose." He picked a bit of skin from his cheek. "You'll have to be fitted for it, of course, and you won't carry half as many as the *Island Lass* over there."

With a small tilt of his head, he showed me where the *Island Lass* lay, and I turned to look, expecting to see a ship as pretty as her name. But I found instead the one that had arrived with the stench and ghastly moans.

"The *Lass* carries nearly a thousand, but I'll tell you, boy..." His lips moved as he read his numbers, loading the ship in his mind. "You might get two hundred in your little hold. A hundred in the fo'c's'le."

"A hundred what?" I asked.

He looked at me as though I were stupid. "Slaves," he said.

"People?" I asked.

"Slaves," said he, as though there were a difference.

The *Dragon's* fo'c's'le was crowded with just our crew of eight. "How do you put a hundred people in there," I asked.

"End to end," he said. "In layers, boy. Pencils in a box."

"They'd suffocate," I said.

He sniffed. "Maybe two in ten."

I thought of the *Dragon* stuffed with men and women, the howls that would come from the hatches. "Get off," I said.

"What?" he asked.

"Get off my ship. Now." I was livid, disgusted just by the sight of the sunburned man. "If I were bigger, I would throw you off," I said.

He blinked at me, peeled-away skin flapping like doubled eyelids. "Now, boy," he said, unruffled. "You need a cargo."

"Not a human one," said I. "I'll carry sugar, but I'll have no part in slavery."

"And who do you think cuts the canes, boy? Who do you think loads the ship but slaves?" He smiled at me. "Whatever you do, boy, you'll be a part of it."

"Then we'll take *no* cargo," I said.

He laughed at the idea, at my foolishness. "Come, come, boy. You don't make money that way."

"And I won't make money *your* way," said I. I drove him from the deck like a great, fat pig and gave him a push to help him over the side. With a squeal he tumbled down to his waiting boat. When I looked away, Abbey was behind me, and he was grinning.

"Good for you," he said. "Good for you, young John."

News of what I'd done spread like a plague through Kingston. When Captain Butterfield came back to the *Dragon* in late afternoon, he knew every detail of it.

"So we're sailing empty," he said. "All the way to Trinidad. Without so much as a ballast stone, is that right?"

"Yes, sir," I said. Slaves loaded ballast stones.

He tried to scowl, but I could see humour in his eyes. "Well, you're as hotheaded as you always were," he said. "As stubborn as your father. But I'll stand by your guns, John, if that's what you want."

"Thank you," I said.

We weighed anchor before the day had ended, passed the English fleet, and headed out to sea. Then we turned to the east and beat our way into the trades. With no cargo, with the guns on her deck, the *Dragon* was more like a boat than a ship. She lay to one side and then to the other, soaked in showers of spray. But the wind was crisp and clean, and revelled in the change.

Jamaica fell astern; Hispaniola rose ahead. And for three wonderful days we followed its shore in a friendly current, as pelicans passed like flocks of flying clowns and dolphins leapt all around us. The sails never needed tending, and men lounged on the deck while I picked away at the little dory's crust. Bits of weed and flakes of white flurried away from my fingers as I worked forward from the spade-shaped transom. I had bared the paint for nearly half her length when Horn came and sat beside me. He took out his knife and started working.

He pressed hard with his blade. It squealed along the wood, lifting a whole strip of growth *and* the paint along with it. "You want to get right down to the planks," he said. "A fresh coat of paint and start anew, that's what you want."

"But I hoped to keep her the way she was," I said.

"No, you don't want that," he told me. "You have to lift all the old paint. Every speck."

I didn't see why. My knife kept scraping, lifting the crust of sea growth, leaving the paint undisturbed. I saw splotches of black on top of the white and knew I was looking at ghosts of old letters, at the name of the ship still borne on her dory. I picked away, baring a letter, baring another.

"Scrape harder," said Horn. He elbowed in where I had been and scraped off all the paint, and the shadows of the letters. "Harder, I tell you." He worked so frantically that his knife nearly took off my fingers. The weeds and the paint flew in a flurry, and the ghostly letters appeared and vanished as his blade flashed along the planks.

"Stop!" I shouted. I pushed at his arm, then brushed away the dried weeds, the flakes of paint. Then I stared in shock at the dory's planks, suddenly knowing why Horn had come to help, why he had tried to scrape off all the paint, why he had never wanted that dory brought aboard at all.

I knew it all, and I glared at Horn.

"It's not what you think," he said.

"Where's the captain?" I asked, turning around.

Horn grabbed my shoulder. "Listen, Mr Spencer. Let me tell you."

"You knew that ship and her crew of mummies," I said. "As soon as you saw her, you knew. You looked back at me because you wondered how much I knew myself."

"No," said Horn. "You don't understand."

He tried to hold me down, but I twisted away, shouting for the captain. In my excitement I cried, "Uncle Stanley!" and faces looked up at the sound of a name they'd never heard, that I hadn't used myself in ten years or more.

Horn had me in his grasp, my wrist in one hand, his knife in the other. But he argued no more, and didn't try to stop me from pulling away. He only bowed his head, let go of my wrist, and put his hand to my brow.

Butterfield ran down from the quarterdeck. Mr Abbey came too, drawn like a shark by the sudden commotion, by any sign of an attack upon Horn. They came and stared at the dory, at the name on her side, the remains of the letters that once had spelled *Meridian Passage*.

Chapter 8

The Black Book

"**S**o that was *your* ship we found," said Butterfield, glaring at Horn. "Your *sunken* ship adrift on the ocean."

"Sir, I said I *believed* she sank," said Horn. "I never said she did."

"And you never said that her men had been murdered. That they'd been triced to the rigging like slaughtered sheep."

"Because I didn't know," said Horn.

"You were on her," snapped Butterfield.

"I wasn't," said Horn. "And I never claimed that I was."

Abbey almost danced a jig. "Spin us another!" he shouted.

"Won't you listen?" said Horn. His great arms bulged

as he tightened his fists. "I saw her at sea, and I gave you her name because I couldn't tell you what ship I was really from."

"And which was that?" asked Butterfield.

Horn's face twisted into something like agony. Then he sighed and said, "The *Prudence*."

"Oh, there's a lovely yarn." Abbey shrieked with his cackling laughter. "He gets caught in his lie and tells us another. He gives us the name of the only ship we can never find to prove him wrong."

Horn glared at the gunner. "What are you saying?" he asked.

It was I who answered. "She's lost," I said. "The *Prudence* has vanished."

"No," said Horn. His brow was deeply wrinkled. "That can't be true."

"Well, it is," cried Abbey. "And you knew it already."

I sided with Horn. "No he didn't," I said.

Horn had been in the rigging when the young lieutenant had come with the news of the missing *Prudence*. He couldn't possibly have known. Then I thought of his ship in the bottle. "That was the *Prudence* you showed me," I said.

Horn nodded, still frowning. "She can't be lost already. There must be some mistake."

"*You're* the mistake," shouted Abbey.

Horn ignored him. He spoke only to me. "It's too soon, John. They're never lost before I make the model."

"You sound as though you meant it to happen," I said.

"The pattern. It's according to the pattern." He seemed confused, then quietly angry. "Well, I hope it's true. I hope she's gone, and that devil's gone with her."

"What devil?" I asked.

He said the name slowly, with a hiss like a snake's. "Bartholomew Grace."

Abbey laughed. "He's spinning yarn!"

"I'm not." Horn raised his fists together, not to strike the gunner but to plead to the captain. "Sir, it's the God's truth," he said, and I could see that it was. No man in the world could lie as convincingly as that.

Butterfield, too, seemed to accept it. "So the *Prudence* is lost?"

"I don't know," said Horn, in an anguished voice. "She was fit and healthy when I left her."

"Then why did you choose to leave her?"

"It wasn't by choice," he said.

"Good God!" the captain roared. "Must you always spin tales?"

Abbey was delighted, but Horn sounded desperate. "Every word is the truth," he said. "I swear it."

"Then how do you explain that dory?"

Horn looked down at the boat. We all did the same, standing beside it like mourners by a casket. It was a long time before Horn spoke. "It's complicated," he said.

Butterfield sighed. For the second time in our voyage I went below with him and Horn, to hear a story as wild as any. We went to the stern cabin, now bright and airy with its open windows, and the captain and I sat at the table like judges at a trial. Horn stood before us, not under the skylight but below the beams, where his height was greater than the overhead. His bent neck and bowed shoulders made him seem small and meek.

"I'm on the run," he said, and so began his tale.

It started in *1778*, when Horn was pressed aboard the *Prudence* to the Indies with Bartholomew Grace for his captain. "A toff," Horn called him; Grace had risen through the ranks like a rocket, from midshipman to post captain in less than ten weeks. "His father was an admiral," said Horn. Then he paused and chewed at his lip.

"The Indies do strange things," he said at length. "The heat, the sun, the wildness of the place. They get inside a soul and twist it up like old rope. They drive some men to madness."

"You?" asked Butterfield drily.

"Bartholomew Grace," said Horn, ignoring that jibe. "He was young and full of fancies about pirates and buried treasure, barely out of boyhood. Sent to the land of the buccaneers, to sink ships and kill men — is it a wonder that he came to think of himself as a pirate?"

"He commanded a warship," said Butterfield.

"But in his mind a pirate ship." Horn smiled. "Piracy was all around us. Where we anchored, the buccaneers had anchored. Their ports of call were ours. He took to pirate ways; you can win a battle before it starts if you fight hand in hand with fear. Fly a bloody flag, come blazing down like a thing from hell, and who won't run from you?"

He paused, and the captain said, "Carry on."

"We did well," said Horn. "We drove the French from the Windward Isles and followed them through the Caribbees. We lived like pirates, from our plunder. Every ship we took was a new suit of sails, a stronger spar, a galley full of food."

Horn shuffled sideways then, and stood to his full height below the skylight, his hands hanging at his sides.

"We lived by the Black Book," he said. "The old laws of Oleron."

"Oh, nonsense," said Butterfield. He leaned back in his chair, staring up at Horn. "The Black Book hasn't been used in centuries."

"Except on the *Prudence*," said Horn.

"It vanished from the High Court—"

"Because he had it." Horn leaned forward, and his big hands lay flat on the table. "Sir, it's the truth. Bartholomew Grace, I tell you, kept that Black Book in his cabin, and he called us down to stand there as he turned through its pages. Every crime you could think of was in there, and for each, a punishment you couldn't imagine. I saw a lookout nailed to the mast when he fell asleep at his post, another tossed overboard for stealing a drink of water. He was a mate of mine, that one. I told

Grace it was murder. I called him a devil, and he took me below. He thumbed through the Black Book until he found what he wanted. He said, 'Ye shall be taken on deck and a rope shall be fixed round thy middle, and ye shall be put over the side and keelhauled.'"

Butterfield scowled. "Is this the truth?"

Without a word Horn turned his back. He lifted the tails of his shirt, and I looked quickly away. I'd seen his scars and didn't care to see them again. But I thought of the horror of how he'd got them, and imagined *myself* being tossed to the sea, being hauled right under the ship as the barnacles cut me like knives and my lungs ached from a want of air.

"Cover yourself, man," said Butterfield. He was very pale, sitting with his hand over his eyes. He waited until Horn turned back, then asked, "But how could this happen? A ship of the British navy."

"The navy made Grace a captain," said Horn. "Nay, it made him a king, with a ship for a kingdom. The wonder is that this didn't happen more often."

"But what happened, exactly?" asked Butterfield.

Horn was tucking in his shirt. "Bartholomew Grace took it into his head that he knew where Captain Kidd's treasure was buried. Why, I think he took it into his head that he *was* Captain Kidd. When the peace came, we poked around the islands for months, until the navy sent us home. It might have ended there, if we hadn't stumbled on the *Meridian Passage*."

"You attacked her," said Butterfield.

"Not I," said Horn. "For three days we followed her, both of us bound for England. Then we had a mutiny of the strangest sort, not the crew against the captain, but the captain against the crew. 'We'll go buccaneering,' said Grace. 'We'll take that ship,' he said. I told him I'd have no part of it, that I'd kill him if he tried. But I was the only one who stood against him — who dared to stand against him — and he bundled me below and read from that cursed Black Book, and set me adrift in the lifeboat. Just me and my sea chest, to rid the ship of all I was."

"And then he attacked the *Meridian Passage?*"

Horn nodded. "Apparently so."

"But an English ship?" Butterfield held up his hands. "It makes no sense."

"It would if you knew him," said Horn. "By that point he hated the English as much as he hated anyone."

"Why?"

"In the last month of the war we were sent to Guadeloupe to sink a French cutter. We were told we'd find a single ship, but instead we found a squadron." Horn closed his eyes. "They knocked the foremast down, and set us afire in the stern. Bartholomew Grace was burned by molten tar, and all the skin was melted from his face and one hand. He believed the English had betrayed him."

Horn's story seemed at last to be complete. I understood why he had stayed so high aloft when the young lieutenant had come with his news of the *Prudence*, why he hadn't gone ashore at Kingston. "You're a deserter," I said.

"Yes, Mr Spencer," said Horn. Then he hesitated. "Well, yes and no. I was cast adrift, so I didn't really desert. But I was in the navy and now I'm not, and that's all the admiralty needs to know to hang me. That's why I was sailing east when you found me. If I'd showed my face in England, the navy would have hanged me. If I'd gone back to the Indies, Grace would have done much worse than that. So I made for Africa, for the Ivory Coast."

"Well," said Butterfield. He pushed back his chair, but didn't get up. "I thank you for your honesty, as slow as it was in coming."

"What will you do with me now?" asked Horn.

The captain looked him straight in the eye. "It's my duty to turn you over to the navy."

I said, "Sir!"

He held up his hand. "It *is* my duty, John. However, I'm not sure if it's the proper course. We shall have to see."

"Thank you, sir," said Horn in the most heartfelt way. He saluted again, with that tiny toss of his hand to his forehead, and he seemed so mild and kind that I thought the world of him then.

We carried on to the east, and the wind grew light. In the evening, fog rolled in, covering the sea in dark swatches of purple and blue. And the night was so utterly black — without a single star and scarcely a swell on the sea — that Horn steered us from sunset to sunrise. Only Horn could steer a ship when there was nothing to steer her by.

At dawn he'd been standing for nearly twelve hours, but he stayed at my side when I took the wheel, and offered words of encouragement as I chased the compass round a quarter of its dial. Then the wind began to rise and slits of sunlight shattered the fog into patches and banks, and we sailed from gloom into sunshine and back into gloom.

The day was just an hour old when the merchantman came. Butterfield stood on my left and Horn on my right, and we saw her rush from a fogbank with all her sails drawing. She changed in an instant from a grey, dim shape to a solid thing in the sun. Then her yards braced back, and she turned away, becoming a ghost again as the next bank of fog closed round her masts.

We were used to seeing ships flee at the sight of us, but this one was different. She seemed stricken with terror — the ship herself driven by panic to run without aim, like a deer from a wolf.

And on her heels came another ship, black as death, with thirty men in the rigging and a spot of bright red at her helm. Painted on her hull was the name *Apostle* and the number *1219*, all crudely — quickly — drawn. At her masthead flapped a ragged flag as black as the ship herself, a white skull grinning.

The men stood along the footropes of the topsail yard, at the crosstrees, in the shrouds. We saw the flash of their cutlass blades, and heard their shouts, softened by the distance to a single voice, an awful wailing like the wind. They rode the ship through skeins of clouds, and at times the hull vanished below them, so that all we saw were those hellish figures racing through the sky. Then that ship, too, passed through the sun and back to the clouds, and only the voices were left.

All three of us trembled with fear, but Horn worst of all. He nearly fell to the deck with shock, and only I knew why. That ship had looked much like the *Dragon*, and I knew her at once as the one that Horn had shown me.

"*Prudence!*" I cried. She was free from her bottle and back from a watery grave.

"Aye," said Horn. "The devil still lives."

"But why does he call his ship *Apostle*?" I asked.

"Who can say what a madman thinks?"

"And those numbers?" asked I. "What does it stand for, twelve hundred and nineteen?"

Horn threw his hands apart in a gesture of bewilderment. Then Butterfield startled us both by slapping hard on the binnacle.

"Not twelve hundred. Just twelve," he said. "Twelve-nineteen. Romans, blast it!"

For a moment I feared that all captains — like gunners — were mad. "I'm sorry, sir," I said.

"Romans: chapter twelve, verse nineteen," said Butterfield.

He made a fist and held it aloft. "'Vengeance is mine; I will repay, saith the Lord.'"

Horn trembled. "God save us," he said.

Chapter 9

Afraid of the Sea

We saw the ships again, one fleeing and the other chasing. We saw them far away, beating to windward, and we sought the thickest of the fogbanks, hiding from the sun and those nightmarish ships. An hour later we heard cannons in the distance, from a bearing that was hard to judge.

Fearing we'd meet the *Apostle*, dreading that we'd stumble on that merchantman and find the same horrors we'd found on the *Meridian Passage*, we turned towards the south, aiming straight for Trinidad across the wide Caribbean. And we were met by a storm like none I'd imagined.

The fog cleared away and the clouds came behind it,

towering up in pillars of black, toppling over, building again. They made spires and walls and great castellated keeps a thousand feet high, like the homes of thunderous giants. And the swells came next, enormous swells with dark and oily faces, so widely spaced that when the *Dragon* balanced on top of one, the next was half a mile away. She laboured up them, balanced at the crests, then raced down their backs with her rail in the water.

Captain Butterfield lashed a weather awning over the skylight and covered his windows again. Then he sat below, wedged in his bunk, with his little lamp sizzling and flaring, with everything he owned — his Bible, his pistol, his books — all swaying and tapping in their places. There he stayed all through that day and into the next, as the wind rose and the waves steepened. Then came the rain, the thunder, and the lightning. With the mainsail triple-reefed, a single jib straining at the bowsprit, we rammed our way towards the south.

The waves boomed against the bow. The wind screamed and shrieked. And the little *Dragon*, with no weight in her hull, was blown like a feather from hither to yon. Now upright, now flat on her side, now pitched across to weather, she tumbled south with Horn at the helm. Only Horn could hold her.

The day turned black as night, the night as black as black can be. When Butterfield came up to the deck in only his nightshirt, he looked like a fluttering ghost that appeared and disappeared in the flashes of the lightning.

He staggered down the deck and wrapped his arms around the binnacle, screaming at Horn, "We have to turn back!"

"We can't," shouted Horn.

I was surprised that the captain would even *think* of turning the ship in those tremendous seas. She could lose her masts or founder in an instant, and if she somehow *did* get her bow to the north, she would surely be dashed to pieces on the shore of Hispaniola.

But he screamed again at Horn. "Turn, I tell you!"

I saw the look of panic on his face and knew that Horn had been right. The captain *was* afraid of the sea. For more than a month he had kept his fear at bay with the curtains of his cabin, but now he could no longer control it.

There was a flash of lightning, a crack of thunder. Butterfield's eyes rolled like those of a horse about to bolt. "Damn you!" he shouted at Horn. He threw himself at the wheel.

Horn was caught by surprise. The spokes whirled through his hands, and the *Dragon* leaned as she turned. The waves rolled over the side and over the deck. They filled the waist until that was all I could see, just a seething of water and masts poking from it, a small group of men who seemed to be swimming.

Butterfield's terror was all that saved us. As the *Dragon* staggered off her course, the blackness on our windward side exploded in flashes of orange and yellow, the sea hurled up spouts of water, and out of the storm — out of the lightning itself — came the *Apostle*.

Before I could move, her black hull ploughed through the crest we had crossed an instant before. Flinging spray, toothed with white water, she came hurtling down the wave and passed close to our stern in a long, black streak and a waft of gunsmoke. Then she climbed from the trough and rolled down to the next, and in an instant she was gone, as though she had never passed at all.

Horn had seen her. He glanced at the sea where the spouts had erupted from the falls of her shot, right where the *Dragon* would have been if it weren't for the sudden turn of the wheel. But for the captain, the flash from her muzzles and the sound of her guns must have seemed like only lightning and thunder, for he kept turning the wheel as the *Dragon* staggered in the seas.

Horn pulled him away. "Take the helm," the sailor shouted to me.

I fought against the ship, against the sails and the rudder and the fury of the wind. A wave broke over the stern, and the water swirled at my knees. But at last the *Dragon* spilled the seas away, flinging herself to weather with a vicious snap.

Butterfield fell at Horn's feet. He lay huddled and white, his arms wrapped around Horn's ankles, his face wretched with fear.

Horn stooped and gathered him up. He spoke very

gently. "Grace is out there. We'll need every hand at the guns, sir."

Butterfield nodded. His teeth were chattering. But he rubbed at his arms and his chest as though patting his pieces — and his wits — back into place. And he managed a smile as he said, "I'll see to it."

He went forward, vanishing in the dark. Horn helped me at the wheel, and we steadied the *Dragon* on a westerly course. She bashed each wave to a cloud of spindrift and corkscrewed over its crest. But a greyness was coming to our world of black, and I saw that dawn was coming. The lightning still flickered, but behind us now, and more distant with every flash. On deck, the group of men at the guns bristled with the handles of sponges and rams.

Behind us came the *Apostle*.

I first saw her by the foam she churned at the bow. A black mass against the sea and the sky, she grew larger every second.

Horn shouted in my ear, "Abbey will need help at the guns."

I started to go, but he pulled me back. "Steer," he said. "And watch her topsail. Grace likes to shoot from the starboard side, so when he braces back, luff up, you hear?"

He left me alone at the wheel — alone in the world, it seemed. There was nothing but shadows beyond the mast, and all around me was the raging sea. The *Dragon* rushed through the storm as fast as her weed-covered hull would let her. And the *Apostle* came bounding behind us.

We pitched over the waves, rising in turn to the crests, always drawing closer. Then I heard the voices of the men that rode her rigging.

Carried by the wind, stretched into terrible wails, they raised the hairs along my neck and sent shivers down my spine. They sounded like voices from the grave, uttering words I could not understand. It was a threat worse than the ship herself, worse than her cannons, and I sang to drown them out.

The only tune that came to mind was Horn's old favourite, "Heart of Oak", and I nearly laughed at the irony of the words as we raced for our lives through the storm: *"Come, cheer up, my lads, 'tis to glory we steer."*

I sang as loudly as I could, screaming out the words, barely taking breaths lest I hear again the voices from the *Apostle*. Soon my song was taken up by the men around the guns, and in the low drone that was all that reached me, the *Dragon* herself seemed to pulse and gather heart.

I let her run, and watched that big, black schooner close the distance. I saw her bowsprit reaching forward, the thin slab of her reefed topsail slashing madly side to side. I saw the ragged men riding on the yard, the foam boiling round the hull. Her bowsprit pierced the seas, rose again, rose and fell as she swiftly overtook us.

I stared at her topsail until my eyes ached. As soon as it moved, the *Apostle* would turn, and all the guns on her starboard side would swing round to face us. I had to bring the *Dragon* about just at that moment, not an instant too soon nor an instant too late.

The waves rolled under us. The jib flapped in the troughs where the wind couldn't reach it, then suddenly filled with a bang and a tug at the wheel.

The *Apostle*'s topsail shivered. I shouted out and turned the wheel. The *Dragon* swung quickly, rearing up on a mountain of water. The *Apostle* rolled as she started her turn. And our two little portside guns blossomed crimson flowers. It was a small sound they made, just a pop in the wind.

I held the wheel down. There was no power in it now, the sails flogging with a din like thunderclaps. A wave burst over the bow, and it seemed she wouldn't come about, that we'd be caught there in irons. "Turn!" I shouted at her.

I waited for the roar of cannons and the crash of balls that would tear our ship to splinters.

But she passed without a shot, so close behind us that I heard the rush of water at her bow. Then our sails filled with wind, and off we went towards the east.

Before I'd caught my breath, the *Apostle* was behind us again.

Chapter 10

A Blood-coloured Banner

We twisted and turned, but the *Apostle* was always there, now astern, now high to windward. Twice she vanished altogether, only to pounce on us from foam-crested waves with her cannons ablaze down her length. A shot whistled through our foremast rigging, snapping shrouds that writhed like serpents. Another tore away the tatters of our ensign, and twice I felt the thump of balls against the hull, counting three hits on our planks, maybe more.

Roland Abbey popped away with his little four-pounders, but we had small hope of hitting her, and none at all of stopping her.

In the full light of day, as the wind began to ease, the

Apostle lay just a mile to windward, close-hauled — as we were — towards the south. I looked across the endless, heaving hills of water and saw only then how high they really were. If I climbed to the topsail yard, I would still not see above them.

Horn and Butterfield and nearly every man aboard had their faces blackened by powder. We all stared at that ship or at the water between us until she rose again into view. We stared at her name and the message of vengeance in the numbers painted starkly on her hull, at the terrible black flag that streamed from her masthead. And we sailed along, the *Apostle* and the *Dragon*, as the sun rose higher.

"What's she waiting for?" I asked Horn when he came to take the wheel.

"For pleasure," he said. His blue eyes burned across the sea. "Have you ever watched a cat with a mouse, the way it bats it about, then sits and waits for it to move? Bartholomew Grace is that way; he gets a pleasure from killing."

"Couldn't we turn back and run for Kingston?" I asked.

Horn shook his head. "Grace would overtake us long before we got there."

"We could sail east and find a harbour in the islands."

"He would follow us."

"Is there nothing we can do?"

"No," said Horn. "Nothing more than put up what fight we can."

For an hour we sailed side by side. The *Apostle* kept a perfect spacing, reefed as we were reefed, to a jib and small main. The waves bore her up, then swallowed her whole.

"Soon now," said Horn.

And the next time she rose, the black flag was gone from her masthead. In its place fluttered a blood-coloured banner.

"The sign of no quarter," said Horn.

Again she vanished in the waves, again she rose, turning towards us now. The crest passed between us; we soared to its back, and there she was, all sails set, rushing straight at us in a fury of foam.

The men were in her rigging, in wind-torn clothes of red and black and gold. But now they rode in silence, and all we heard was the ship: the creaking of her rudder and planks, the flutter of her topsail. She came fast — incredibly fast — the reefs shaken out of her sails. Abbey tended to his guns, but it seemed hardly worth the bother. He could throw just eight pounds of iron at a ship weighing two hundred tons. His glass eye glowing, his round head wrapped in its scarlet cloth, he went about his business with all the bravery of Nelson. Wedges were driven to lower the barrels; the flintlocks were armed, and men took up the lanyards — Mudge at one, Abbey himself at the other.

"Wait for it now," he said.

The *Apostle* bounded towards us. The foam at her bow

tumbled along. Thirty men rode her rigging, and her deck was crowded with figures.

Abbey fired first, and the ball fell short. With a hopeless little spout it buried itself yards before her bowsprit.

Horn steered calmly down a wake as straight as a spar. My old uncle Stanley, beside him, tried to seem nonchalant, but his fright showed in his eyes, and in his hands, which went constantly from his side to his collar to his thin hair, made into sodden curls by rain and spray. For me, it was almost too much to bear. The black ship came so swiftly, so purposefully, and we were so helpless against her that I wanted to run and hide somewhere. I thought of the ship we had seen, decorated with dead men, and I felt the scratch of a noose at my neck. I turned away, to hide the tears that came to my eyes.

I stared forward, at Abbey and his guns. It struck me that he really had seen the future with his coffin in the sea, that we had all been doomed from that moment on. Through tears I looked at the bowsprit, down the leeward rail, across the waves that swept away towards a land I would never see again. I watched the waves toss and roll — a huge, uncaring sea. And I saw a sail atop it.

It grew in an instant to a pyramid of sails, and a hull appeared below it, bobbing on the swell. A big, slow ship, she made her way north under canvas whitened by the sun. And I knew then why the *Apostle* was hurrying so, why her men were silent; she wasn't after us at all.

I spun to face that black ship. In the minute that I'd looked away, she'd come seven times her length towards us. Her bowsprit towered up; the men looked down from the ratlines and the yard.

"By the guns!" I shouted. "Hold your fire."

Horn looked towards me. Butterfield too.

"She'll pass us by," I said.

But Abbey was already tugging on his lanyard. And the four-pounder barked out smoke.

Splinters flew from the *Apostle*'s stern. A chunk of her rail was suddenly gone, and a dreadful scream rose from her crowded deck.

She'll turn on us now, I thought. Like a lion we had poked with a stick, she would attack in a blind rage and shred us with her claws.

But the hull kept passing. Her name, her numbers marched on by. The guns kept passing, though five men stood at each, naked to the waist, ready with their sponges and their rams. Then her quarterdeck came level with our stern, the shattered railing passing, and I saw a dead man on the deck, another bleeding from the chest. Above them, at the helm, stood Bartholomew Grace.

There was no one else it could be. Tall, strong, elegant-looking, he wore a gold-trimmed coat and a gold-trimmed hat with a crimson plume in its crown. He steered with one hand, looking ahead, and the wide brim of his hat fluttered round his face.

Then he turned towards us. Gliding past, he turned his

head. He took his hand from the wheel and swept off his hat, stooping into a courtly bow. One knee bent, his black hair tumbling in tangled ringlets, he saluted us as our ships sailed on and parted. And when he lifted his face, it seemed at first as though he *had* no face. It was featureless, pale, just a mouth and a pair of dark eyes, and I remembered what Horn had told me. *Burned by molten tar.*

Then he was gone, travelling off towards those distant sails. The hat was back on his head, his hand on the wheel again. And the great, bloody flag rippled above him.

Butterfield looked to leeward, towards the tower of white sails. "So that's it," he said. "We're saved at the cost of those poor devils there."

"Maybe," said Horn. "If we're lucky."

"But we've got no cargo," said I. "We're just an empty schooner."

"Full of powder and shot," said Horn. "Grace always needs ammunition, new sails and new masts. If he decides to take them from us, then nothing will stop him."

"We'll set a new course," said Butterfield. "As soon as we've put the horizon between us."

"Do what you please, it wouldn't make any difference." Horn's pigtail swayed across his shoulders as he lifted his head. "If he decides to chase us, you might as well strike the colours right now, and say your prayers while you can, for he'll catch us in the end. Turn east and you'll find him there. West, and that's where he'll be."

"He's only a man," said Butterfield.

"No, he's more than that," said Horn. "Or less than that."

He gazed towards the *Apostle*, but his eyes were fixed on the distance. The merchantman lumbered along on her course, not yet in any fear or hurry.

"Grace is everything we're not," said Horn. "He has venom for blood. He's had us stalk a ship for days, towing barrels off the stern to slow us down, to let some lot of poor sailors think they might just get away."

"Then why do we run?" I asked. "We might as well turn and fight him now."

Horn put his hand on my shoulder. "Don't be in such a hurry, lad. By and by, your time will come."

Chapter 11

The fever

The wind was too strong for our topsail, but we set it nonetheless. We raised the foresail and took the reefs from the main; we set a gaff above it. We bent on nearly every sail that we had in our hurry to leave the *Apostle* behind.

No longer did we sing "Heart of Oak", or any song at all. We felt like cowards, like traitors. When the sound of cannon fire reached us, faint as finger taps, we all pretended not to hear. Butterfield wrote in his log that day, "Sighted an unknown ship to leeward. God save their souls."

For nearly three hours we battered along on our course. When the sea was utterly empty, we turned sharply to the south, hiding in the waves like a mouse in a meadow.

We ran and we ran, the poor *Dragon* groaning as though from pain. She rolled so fast and so far that three men came down with the seasickness, slumping on the deck with their faces green as limes. And with each roll, we heard a gurgle and a splutter from the hull, as seawater made its way in through the *Dragon*'s wounds.

So we pumped as we ran. And it was two days before the sea settled enough to let Abbey go over the side.

He sat in the loops of a Spanish bowline, and we lowered him from the rail. With the sea at his feet, and then at his shoulders, he prodded and banged at the planks. "Forward!" he shouted. Or, "Aft!" And we shuffled him back and forth until he let us know, with a cry, that he had found the damage done by the *Apostle*'s cannons.

I watched for sharks as he worked down there, hidden by the curves of the hull. Then, "Up!" he shouted, and a moment later he was sitting exhausted on the deck, his old face alarmingly red from his effort. We stood round him, solemn as priests.

"They hit us twice," he said.

"I counted three," I said. "Maybe four."

"Well, they *hurt* us twice. Far as I can see," said Abbey. "In one place the planks are stove in. And just below here" — he slapped the deck — "there's a ball stuck in the hull like a cork."

"Can we repair it?" asked Butterfield.

"We can patch it." Abbey coughed. He spat out a dribble of seawater. "But we'll have to do more than that before we load at Trinidad."

Again he went over the side, and he plugged the holes with canvas and tar. But still the sea came in. We were pumping for an hour in every watch by the time we sighted the old Spanish Main ten days out from Jamaica. Butterfield went down to uncurtain his windows, and with trees and green hills at our side, we worked our way east. By day we beat into the trades, and at night we rode breezes that smelled of rivers and jungles.

But the leak quickened in the hull until, pumping both night and day, we worried that we'd sink before we ever got to Trinidad. Abbey said, as though the thought were his own, that a third shot must have hit us. "We'll have to dry her out," he said.

Horn knew a place, a broad beach at a river's mouth on the shore of Venezuela. It had been used for centuries, he said, by the Spaniards and the buccaneers. Then he clapped me on the shoulder. "You might even find doubloons in the sand," he said, grinning ear to ear.

It was a lovely bay he took us to, the sort of place I'd always conjured in my mind whenever I'd thought of the Indies. Coconut trees leaned over a strip of silver sand, their huge fronds spread like parasols. At the head of the bay, mangroves lined the shore, standing on their roots as though they sought to climb above the water. Beyond them was a chaos of green: trees and vines and ferns all tangled in a mass. And the river twisted from the vegetation, brown as dirt, like a living snake coming from the dank, green thickness.

A burst of bright-coloured birds rose at the dropping of our anchor. We furled the sails, then flocked ashore like children. Some swam, some took the boats, but all of us went. Or all but Horn. He rigged a hammock for himself between the shrouds and the foremast, and put an awning above it. There he slept, in the shade, planning to dream — he said — of native girls.

We played bowls with coconuts; we splashed in water warmed by sun. I dug in the sand but found no doubloons. It would have been a paradise if it hadn't been for the hordes of flies.

I had never seen anything like them in England. Long-legged things, armed with spikes that sucked our blood, they flew with a high and irritating whine in clouds about our heads. Abbey called them mosquitoes. They drove us from the beach in the end, and we set to work to heel the *Dragon* down.

We shifted the cannons all to one side, then stretched a line from the capstan to the masthead and down to a mangrove that was as thick as a barrel. The tree's trunk was ringed by scars, the marks of ropes, like those I'd once seen round the neck of a man who had been hanged. Most of the rope marks were ancient but some were very new, and we spaced our own lines between them. Then we hauled round the capstan, and the *Dragon* lay on her side like a great wooden beast.

Uncle Stanley took it into his head that he would like to catch a parrot to take home to England. So he set off up the river in the dory, with dimwitted Mudge to row, as I and the others scraped the schooner's hull.

We peeled away acres of grass, tons of thick-shelled barnacles, mussels, and squirting sponges that popped under our feet. Abbey found the source of our leak: a shattered plank far below the waterline. "Well, you were right," he said when he took me there to see it. "Only a cannonball could have done this." He knelt on the round of the hull and pressed his fist against the plank. He could nearly push right through it.

"You see?" he said. "They hit us three times."

"Or more," I said.

"No, only three." He looked up at me, his good eye closed against the sun. "Unless there's something on the other side."

"No," I said. All our hits, I thought, had been to starboard.

"Well, we'll have a look," he said.

Abbey tore away his patches, then chiselled out the broken planks and fitted new ones into place. He hammered oakum down the seams, the clang of his iron ringing through the trees, so that the birds never rested, but flew round and round the jungle in a huge and glittering wheel. Then a bit of paint, a bit of tallow, and the *Dragon* — or half of her, at least — was as strong as the day she was built.

The next day we careened her on the other side and scraped the growth from there. Abbey tapped at every plank, but we could see at a glance that the hull was sound. And the *Dragon* was already floating when the captain and Mudge returned from their second trip up the river.

I couldn't help smiling to see them coming. The boat could seat two oarsmen, but Mudge lolled in the stern while my uncle Stanley did the rowing, as lazily as a man ever rowed. Between them was what seemed at first to be a parrot but was only a collection of feathers stuck into half a coconut, arranged to look like a bird. And they came so slowly — barely faster than the river itself — that they looked like a pair of boys at the end of a grand adventure. They were the best of friends; I could see that now. Though Butterfield cursed poor Mudge at every turn, he was very fond of the sailor.

They came aboard laughing, scratching themselves, nearly eaten alive by mosquitoes. Mudge carried the coconut parrot as carefully as he would have held a real bird. He smoothed its feathers as Butterfield looked on. Then he gave it to the captain, with a little show of embarrassment and the kindliest smile I'd ever seen.

"What are you grinning at?" Butterfield asked me. "Hoist the boat aboard and make sail."

The *Dragon* leaked not a drop as we sailed along on our way. "Tight as a drum," said Abbey, eager to lord over me that he'd been right and I'd been wrong. He was still gloating when we fetched the shores of Trinidad.

At Port of Spain, on the northwestern tip of the island, we loaded our cargo of sugar and coffee. Sacks weighing half a hundredweight filled the holds, packed on a bed of coconut husks. The carved dragon at the bow sank lower and lower, as though trying to drink from the harbour water. Then the hatches were sealed, and we cast off for the long voyage home.

Where we'd struggled before, we now ran with the wind, the glorious trades sweeping us on under sunshine or glittering stars. We passed Grenada and the Grenadines, up the chain of islands at the edge of the Caribbean Sea. Then Mudge came aft, early on a morning, to take my place at the helm. And the next in a chain of troubles fell upon us.

He was shaking, sweating. His eyes were full of fear.

"What's wrong?" I asked.

"I don't know." He shook like a wet dog, and held himself about the shoulders. "I'm cold as death. My head's about to burst, I think."

He swayed on his heels, then grabbed my shoulder to steady himself. His hand felt hot as fire.

"Fetch the captain, John," he said. "Fetch him fast; I think I'm dying." He reeled sideways and fell in a faint to the deck.

I turned and stared through the skylight. Butterfield sat at the table, hurrying to get through his breakfast.

When I stamped on the framed glass, he looked up, startled, with a bit of buttered biscuit pinched between his fingers.

"Come up!" I shouted. "It's Mudge. He's fainted."

"*Fainted?*" Butterfield mouthed the word so plainly that I heard his voice in my head. Then he shot up from the table and vanished from the skylight, rattling up the companionway an instant later, with the biscuit still in his hand. He dropped on the deck beside Mudge as others came from the waist and the fo'c's'le, drawn by the sudden commotion, to stand in a circle around us. Horn was last, but he cleared a path with his arms, right to the front of the small crowd.

Butterfield took his old friend in his arms. "Dana," he said, and lifted Mudge's head from the deck.

I saw bumps on the sailor's neck, balls of flesh standing out.

"What's wrong with him?" asked Butterfield.

"He said he's dying," said I.

My uncle looked at me bleakly. "Dying?"

Horn laughed. "He's not dying." He nudged his foot at Mudge's ribs. "Get up, man. Pull yourself together."

"Leave him," said Butterfield. He pushed at Horn's foot. "What do you know of it?"

"I know he's got the fever, is all." Horn, too, knelt on the deck. He pinched Mudge's cheeks — rather roughly, I thought. But Mudge came awake, and blinked up at the faces all around him.

"It's all right," said Butterfield. "You're not dying, you muttonhead."

"But he'll hope he will," said Horn. "He'll get the shivers and then the aches, and he'll be out of his head for days. That's what comes from mucking about in swamps."

An odd look came over Butterfield's face. There was relief there, but dread as well. He had also been "mucking about in swamps".

We packed Mudge down to the captain's cabin. The curtains were only half closed, as the islands were still pale shapes in the east. Mudge lay in the shade, with Butterfield for his nurse. Just as Horn had predicted, the fever took hold of him.

A rash spread over his skin. Every joint in his body ached to the point that it hurt him just to lie still. The bumps of flesh appeared in other places, and he dreamed troubling dreams that made him thrash about, then wake screaming from the pain.

A second man came down with it, then a third, then another. By evening all three men lay moaning in their fo'c's'le hammocks, and Mudge in the stern. The sounds of despair filled the ship from fore to aft.

Our crew reduced by half, we stood extra tricks at the wheel. And at sunset, as I steered the *Dragon* north, I felt every little twitch and twinge in a way I'd never felt before, sure that I'd be next to succumb to the fever.

It was nearly dark when Horn came to take my place.

He brought us up a point to windward, and I felt a sluggish rolling in the hull as the *Dragon* gained a knot of speed. He put a peg in the traverse board to mark the change in course, then raised his head to choose a star to steer towards.

"The fo'c's'le's like a furnace," he said. "And your gunner's down there, all in a sweat, wondering why he's hot." Horn laughed. "He's scared he's got the fever."

His humour annoyed me. "Why shouldn't he be?" I asked.

Horn shrugged. "I might be too, if I were an old gunner with my brains blown away. I've seen ships drifting, all sheets to the wind, with not a man aboard fit to tend a sail."

"That could happen to us."

"It won't," he said.

"Why not?"

"You don't catch the fever from your shipmates, Mr Spencer. You catch it from the swamps and jungles; it's in the air, you see."

"We were *all* in the jungle," I said.

"Well, not quite."

"No," said I. "Not you."

He looked up at his star. "The helm feels heavy," he said.

I ignored him. "Why didn't you go to shore? What kept you on the ship?"

"The fates, I suppose," said Horn. He smiled in the darkness. "I've told you before: I'm blessed."

I heard a groan from the cabin below, then Butterfield's voice: "Hush now, hush."

Horn kept his hands on the wheel. "I'm like your guardian angel," he said.

Chapter 12

To Davy Jones

Horn was still at the helm when I came up from my berth in the hours close to dawn. The wind had fallen, and the sails drew lazily as the *Dragon* ghosted along. Horn, I fancied, could keep her moving in no wind at all.

"Have you been steering all night?" I asked.

"It's no bother to steer," he said. "She's a lovely ship, Mr Spencer."

I had a sense of having been there before, as though we'd spoken the same words at a time I couldn't quite remember. But then I heard the groaning from the fo'c's'le, and it seemed to me that more men had been taken by the fever.

"She seems heavy tonight," said Horn for the second

time during his watch. "I sounded the bilges, but they're dry as dust. It's odd."

I stood still beside him, listening to the sails and the rigging, trying to feel the motion of the schooner.

"Here." Horn stepped from the wheel. "See what you think."

I took the spokes in my hands. I turned them and felt the rudder pushing at the water. Was it just the thought that she was heavier that now made the helm feel different? I wasn't convinced.

"I don't know," I said, looking back.

Horn had moved away. He stood at the rail, leaning so far over the side that I could easily have tipped him overboard. The thought actually occurred to me. I even saw myself doing it; just a push and he would tumble over. Then I gripped the spokes as hard as I could, for it scared me to see that picture in my mind. I didn't *want* to tip him over, and had never even dreamed of it.

The man's an albatross, Abbey had said. *He's a Jonah.* But I hadn't believed it then, and didn't believe it now. I remembered the gunner's sighting of a coffin, and his dream. *We'll see a rain of iron, a flood, a pestilence, and a fire.*

My arms began to tremble, so hard did I hold the wheel. Abbey's dream was coming true: we had been shot at, nearly sunk, and attacked by a plague of mosquitoes. All that he had foretold had come to pass. Except the fire.

But I drove those thoughts from my mind. They had

nothing to do with Horn, I told myself. They were just the ideas of an addled old gunner.

Horn straightened at the rail. "She's down in the water," he said.

"How much?" I asked.

"Come and see for yourself."

I lashed the wheel in place and hurried to the rail. The brightness of the stars and the blackness of the sea nearly made me dizzy, as though I were balanced at the edge of space with only a void below me. But when I leaned farther over the rail, I saw the water shimmering against the planks, bright feathers and bubbles of green spinning past the hull.

"She's down an inch," said Horn. "Maybe two."

I couldn't tell the difference, but Horn had a better feel for the ship, a sense of her ways that I had envied from the beginning. I had to go up to the bow and out onto the sprit before I could see for myself. I watched the carved dragon taking bites at the sea — the water exploding into green around its teeth — and saw that he was right. The wooden jaws bit too deeply at the water. They barely spat a mouthful out before they dipped and took another. It was true; the *Dragon* was slowly sinking.

Horn went back to the wheel. I stopped in the waist and sounded the bilge. But the pole came up without a trace of water, and I could make no sense of it.

At dawn, we were both still at the wheel, both silent as

we puzzled it out. The *Dragon* was growing heavy, but no water was sloshing about in the bilge. Not a drop, I thought. That was odd in itself, for every ship took on water, and there had always been half a foot or so slopping over the keelson. But now it seemed — quite impossibly — that the *Dragon* leaked it *out*. Or our cargo had somehow grown bigger. Or heavier.

"Coconut husks!" I shouted.

Horn frowned at me.

"The husks are sopping up water."

I went down to my cabin and fetched the lamp from its holder. In its warm, smoky glow I went crawling through the ship, squirming to the depth of the hold. There I found bags chewed away at the corners and heard the rats retreating before me. Down I went, down to the bottom, where water — too low and too hidden for even the sounding pole to find — slobbered and slopped in a sinister way. I could hear it coming into the ship, creeping over frames and ribs. My hand touched a sugar bag that was cold and wet, and the one beside it was the same, and the ones above them and below them too. And underneath, the coconut husks were as sodden as sponges.

I might have traced the wetness in the bags, and discovered where the hull was leaking. But all I could think of was climbing from the hold, away from the slop of the water and the dizzying roll of the ship and — worst of all — the squeal of the rats that raised terrible memories of my father's ordeal at the hands of the Cornish wreckers. I hurried away in such fear and haste that my lamp was still burning when I came up to the deck, to sunshine and a freshening breeze.

The captain was there, and Horn, and Abbey in the same old cloak I'd first seen him wearing. They leaned towards me with worried looks, as though I were a doctor bringing news from a sickroom.

I told them what I'd found: twenty sacks, at the least, ruined by the water. "We have to shift them out," I said. "The whole lot. We have to empty the hold, then stop the leak."

"With half the crew too sick to work?" asked Butterfield. He balled his hands into fists and knocked them together. "What if we ran for England, straight for home?"

"The cargo wouldn't be worth a penny," I said. "I can't let my father down."

He frowned and nodded. "Then we'll have to go back to Kingston. The dockyard there will do it."

"Too far," said Horn. "If we run to Kingston, we'll have to go on, clear to the Tortugas, or beat to windward all the way back. Put her on a beach, sir; that's what I would do."

"There's Antigua," I said. "It's closer."

But again Horn argued. "We'll have to beat through the Leeward Islands," he said. "Do you know where the reefs are? Where the sandbanks are?"

"The chart will show them," said I.

"Some, perhaps. Not all." Horn was dead set on his own idea. "A beach, sir. Just turn to the sun."

Butterfield looked to the east, where the morning sun rose over the chain of cloud-wreathed islands. We could fetch them in a day: by morning at the latest. "But where?" he asked.

Horn's blue eyes stared at the compass. He didn't even bother to glance at the land. "I know a place," he said.

Abbey laughed scornfully. "I'm sure you do."

Butterfield reddened. "Mr Abbey!" he said.

"Well, didn't he steer us to a place where half the crew might catch the fever?" said Abbey. "Didn't he steer us to that dead men's ship? Didn't he have the helm when the *Apostle* found us?"

"That's enough!" shouted Butterfield.

"He's a Jonah, I tell you."

"Now listen, *Mister* Abbey." Butterfield pointed a finger at the gunner. "My ship is leaking, my cargo's going to ruin, half my crew are sick as dogs, and if Horn knows a place where we can get this repaired, that's good enough for me."

Abbey turned to me. "Tell him, John. Tell him what I dreamed."

"The devil take your dreams!" shouted Butterfield. And he too appealed to me. "John, are you willing to let Horn lead us?"

Why it was put on *my* shoulders, I didn't understand. Perhaps the captain was having doubts of his own, for it was true that Horn had always steered us to our troubles. Wherever he took us, bad luck followed, as though he had the devil for his shadow. I looked at Horn, and he seemed very sad, so melancholy that I almost pitied him. But I dreaded to think where he might take us next, and I let the gunner have his way. I said, "*I* know a place. And it's right over there."

"Where?" asked Butterfield.

I lifted my hand, surprised to find the lantern still dangling from it. I pointed vaguely towards the east. In truth, I had no idea what lay among the islands there, but I was sure I could look at the charts and pick a spot. And I decided I would rather do that than follow Horn to his choice.

"Come below," said Butterfield. "You and Abbey, come below."

We went down to the cabin and found it so gloomy that I saw only then that my lamp was still burning. Poor Mudge huddled on the captain's bunk, and the light that I carried fell across his face. The rash had spread over his yellowed skin, which was so bright with sweat that he looked like a great, oozing slug. And he moved no more quickly than that as he raised a hand and mumbled something at us.

There was a bucket on the deck beside him, a sponge floating on the surface. He groaned most pitifully.

"Maybe he wants his decks swabbed down," said Abbey.

I stepped closer, hoping to help. I lifted the lamp, and Mudge mumbled more loudly.

Butterfield was bent over his table, his back towards me. "It's frightfully dark in here," he said. "But the light sends swords through his eyes, the poor soul."

"Oh," I said, chagrined. I took the lamp to the table, and Mudge settled back into a restless sleep.

"So where's this island of yours?" asked Butterfield.

We stared at a maze of little islands, each one as foreign to me as Siberia. I had hoped to see a place where the water was shallow and sand-bottomed, sheltered from the trades. But that hope was dashed on the instant, for Butterfield had chosen a chart that showed all of the Caribbean Sea, and the islands were no bigger than peas.

"Just point it out," he said.

I moved my hand across the chart. "Now, let me think."

"Come, come. We're not as far to the south as that," the captain said. "Here's where we be."

He put his finger on the chart in the curve of the Leeward Islands. The lamp made a huge, black shadow behind it. And I saw with dismay that my hand hovered over a spot nearly half a thousand miles away.

I moved it quickly north, up the chain of islands. But I could see it was no use; I couldn't hope to pick a spot. We would have to go wherever Horn might choose.

But Abbey came to my rescue. "I know where the lad is thinking of," he said. "It's here." He touched a big finger to the tangled islands just east of our position. "It's called Culebra — isn't it, John? — and it's as fine a careenage as you'd hope to see."

I looked at him, his face shadowed in the lamplight.

"Yes," I said. "That sounds right."

Butterfield laughed. "You surprise me, the pair of you," he said. "I didn't think you'd carry your game as far as this." He lifted the chart, and underneath it was the one I'd hoped to see, showing the islands in all their detail. "Now, where's this Culebra?"

Abbey pointed it out, and it was a wonderful island with a deep and sheltered harbour, and beaches on the western shore, all ringed by coral reefs.

"You've been there before?" asked the captain.

"Yes," said Abbey.

"Very well," said Butterfield. "Go and tell Horn to steer for Culebra." He got his rulers out and marched them to the compass rose. "Tell him to steer nor'east."

Horn met me at the deck with one of his long and burning looks. "Well?" he asked. "What's it going to be?"

"Steer nor'east," I said. "We're going to Culebra."

I saw his jaw tighten. "Whose idea was that?"

"It's the captain's decision," I said.

"Is it?" asked Horn. "I would have thought it was Roland Abbey's."

How he guessed that, I couldn't imagine. But I wouldn't give him the satisfaction of knowing he was right.

"I'll steer to Davy Jones if I'm told to," said Horn. He

turned the wheel and began to bring the *Dragon* round. "And if you ask me, Mr Spencer, that's just where we'll be going."

Chapter 13

Show No Quarter

We came upon Culebra from the south, just as dawn was breaking. Ahead, and off our beam, the big Atlantic swells hurled themselves against the reefs with enormous spouts of creamy froth. And all around us was a deep and throaty roar, a silver mist of spray.

It was a small island, dark and mysterious, a hunch of green spotted by six pale hills, steep-sided and round, like the warts on the back of an enormous toad. In the spray and the dim of the dawn, it somehow bore a sense of ill-thought that a tragedy had happened here, that the trees and the hills remembered a horror, that the island — somehow — was waiting for us.

The current ran fast, ebbing to the east, sweeping us

closer to the off-lying rocks and the wild spouts of shattered waves. We had to turn, and turn again, to keep ourselves on course. And every time we turned, the island seemed to slide to the east, as though tempting us to chase it.

On the wind came a smell of weeds and poisoned rock, of surf on battered shores. It was a thick, foul odour, and Butterfield hunched his shoulders against it. He held a spyglass, which he rapped on his palm. "I don't like this," he said. "It seems an evil place."

"Evil it is," said Horn. "That's Davy Jones you're smelling."

"It's a rookery you're smelling," said Abbey. "That's all that is." He was our pilot, but Horn was the helmsman. And it was clear to us all that Horn knew the waters well. He met every surge of current, every breaking wave, a moment before they touched us.

"You've been here before," I said.

Horn nodded. "Yes."

"Many times?"

"A few." He turned the wheel, and the *Dragon* rocked in a swift eddy. "These were Kidd's islands. He buried his treasure somewhere here, then sailed up to New York with just a few chests of gold, hoping to buy his freedom."

Abbey smirked. "You tell us, Spinner," he said.

"It's not a yarn," said Horn. "It's the truth I'm telling you. We took the longboat to every cay and every island, and the sun burnt the oarsmen to cinders. Aye, there's treasure here, and death as well."

"Go on!" cried Abbey.

"You watch for that black ship," said Horn. "You're as likely to find her here as anywhere."

Abbey laughed. But there was no gaiety in it. "Then we're more likely *not* to find her here, aren't we?"

"Enough!" said Butterfield. He stepped between the pair as though prying them apart with his spyglass. "If you've really been to Culebra, Mr Abbey, please tell me: what *will* we find?"

"Water," said the gunner. "Good, fresh water, sir. A place to careen the ship, and timber if we need it. A place to let Mudge and the others get ashore before another hour passes and another sack of sugar goes to ruin."

Butterfield scowled at the shore. "It seems a most unpleasant place."

"But safe," said Abbey. "Safe as houses."

I saw what he meant. The rocks and reefs that made our approach so treacherous would protect us once we had passed them. They would stand guard like watchmen, and let us see any vessel coming in our path.

"I vote for Culebra," I said.

Butterfield smiled. "When did seamen get the vote?"

"I mean we don't have much choice," I said, blushing. "We can stand off the harbour and—"

"I know what you meant." He put his hand on my shoulder. "I think you're right, John. Let's carry on, shall we?"

We shortened sail and readied the anchor. Harry

Freeman took soundings, shouting his depths above a steady thrum of surf. The bottom came up from twelve fathoms to seven, then sharply to three. But Horn was unruffled, and with a touch of the wheel he brought us back to deep water.

The harbour opened before us, battered by surf at its entrance but peaceful and calm beyond that. It was somehow sad and lonely, and we were greatly surprised to see the masts of a ship that was anchored in there.

"A brig," I said, squinting. "English, by the look of her."

"Navy?" asked Horn.

"I don't think so."

Butterfield pressed his spyglass into my hands. "Your eyes are sharper than mine," he said.

I took it up and studied the little ship. Her yards were crossed, but not as neat as navy fashion. They were stripped of all sails, as though she had settled down for a long stay. Anchored at the bow, moored at the stern, she lay at a slant beyond the narrows, pulled by the ebbing tide.

"Anyone aboard?" asked Butterfield.

"Yes," I said. Three men stood watch, one on the main yard and one by the capstan, another at the wheel with his arms spread wide across the spokes. They seemed the most idle, shiftless crew; not one raised a hand or gave any sign that he saw us.

Then the ship was blotted out in my lens, hidden by the land again, and I snapped the spyglass shut. I was happy to think we wouldn't be alone.

Butterfield had the anchor dropped, and we sat to wait for the change in tide. It was at least an hour away, and the *Dragon* rocked so uncomfortably in the swells, and the fevered men moaned so pitifully, that I made an excuse to get off her. I volunteered to row the dory in with a line I could tie to shore.

"I can have it all ready," I told Butterfield. "We can warp her right to the beach."

As always, my uncle Stanley knew what I was really thinking. "If I were young and eager, I'd be anxious to go ashore too," he said. "Well, off you go, and if you *happen* to speak to that brig, give my compliments to the captain."

"Yes, sir," I said.

I launched the dory, tossed in a coil of line, and then nearly broke my back rowing against the tide. It flowed from the harbour with the strength of a small river, whipped by the wind into quick little waves that seemed to leap from the sea and into the boat. I soon had water up to my ankles, but I kept on rowing, for it was easier than stopping. I drifted back a foot for every yard I gained, was flung to my left and then to my right, until at last I passed the narrows and found the rowing easier.

I could see the bottom then, five fathoms down. Bright-coloured fish flitted over sand that was white as silver, rippled by the current into tiny hills and valleys. I watched them as I rowed along, whole schools dashing past, dashing back, turning like a single animal. Suddenly they rose, and swarmed towards the dory. They came from either side, from ahead and behind, packing into the shadows of my little boat. There were so many fish that I could hear the ticking of their tiny fins against the planks. At first I was delighted.

Until I saw the shark.

It passed deep below, moving with a languorous twisting of its body. From head to tail it was twenty feet long, and in the slow twitching of its gills, in the lazy curving of its body, I saw such sinister purpose that it turned my blood to ice.

Just as quickly, it was gone. The fish darted back into the sunbright water, and I dug in the oars to hurry along.

Again the fish bunched at the boat. And behind me came the shark.

It was on the surface now, its curved fin slicing through the sea, rushing up the path or ripples that my oars had made. Steadily it came, a curl of water pushed before it, faster and faster, until it seemed it meant to cleave my boat in two. Then, inches from the stern, that wicked fin disappeared. And with a thrashing of its tail, a vicious swirl of water, the shark thumped against the boat and tipped it onto its side.

I grabbed for the gunwale, then reached frantically for an oar that was slipping through its pins. All the water in the boat weighed it down, and I feared it wouldn't come upright. Another thump, harder than before — hard enough to crack the wood — tossed the dory onto her other side. A second shark passed below the boat.

Suddenly there were three fins circling round and round my dory. The little fish clung to her shadows. I banged my oars on the pins, trying to scare the sharks' food away, but they only tightened below me, like children at a mother's skirt. Full of terror, my heart pounding, I rowed harder than I ever had.

There was one more thump — at the bow, behind me. Something cold and hard scraped against my shoulder. I screamed, and raised my hands to push against it. The oars slid out and sailed away. And my arms closed on a cable, the great, thick rope that anchored the brig in the harbour.

I was so startled that I thrust it away. The dory spun past, under the bowsprit, and nudged against the brig's cutwater. I scrambled for a handhold before the current could catch the boat and sweep me out again. But the rigging was too high above me, and my hands only scratched at the planking.

I shouted for help, but not a man came to save me. With utter desperation I stood on the dory's thwart, balanced myself as it rocked and tipped, then leapt for the rigging.

I drove the dory under. It sank with a burble of air, then rolled upside down. And I dangled from the bobstay, staring down as a shark came flitting over the sandy bottom and, rising in a grey streak, ripped the dory in half.

The knowledge that no man was offering to help me

spurred me on to help myself. I found enough strength to swing up my legs and wrap them round the bobstay. Then I pulled myself along it, and over the rail to the deck.

I lay on my back, panting like a dog. High above me stood the man on the mainyard, his head tipped down, his hands behind him to hold the mast. But he only stared; he made no effort to help me.

The man at the wheel was the same. His arms still spread across the spokes; he hadn't moved at all since the first time I'd seen him. Then I rolled onto my side and saw the man at the capstan, as uncaring as the others.

"Won't you help me?" I asked "Won't anyone help me?" but he didn't even turn his head.

I got up and started towards him. I staggered from exhaustion, but made it close enough so that I could see him more properly. Then the horror of what I saw made me forget my own pains. The man was dead. He was nailed to the capstan.

I reeled away, going aft towards the wheel. I passed the mainmast and, glancing up, saw that the lookout there was dead as well, fixed to the mast by a great spike driven through his chest. I didn't bother going up to the quarterdeck, for I saw the dried blood that caked the helmsman's hands, and didn't want to go any closer than that to a man crucified to a wheel.

Panic struck me. I felt it in my legs and in my head, a dark rushing of blood that at once emptied me and filled me.

The brig rocked in a swirl of currents. The land slid past her shrouds and her masts, and I sensed that the tide was changing. When I whirled around towards the harbour entrance, I saw the *Dragon* with her sails set, hauling off towards the south.

"Wait!" I screamed. "Wait!" But it was futile. I could imagine Abbey and Butterfield looking over the side and seeing my dory float past, in shards and splinters. I could understand their thinking I'd been lost to the waves or the sharks. But I couldn't possibly imagine why they'd weigh anchor and give me up as soon as this.

A new rush of horror swept through my veins at the thought that I was now marooned on a ship manned by corpses. My own shouts seemed to echo in my head, for there was no sound at all in that wicked place. The ship was silent, and a stillness hung over the island. Not even a bird moved through the trees or the sky. The island was like a living thing — a beast with its breath the distant surf — that had risen and struck, and now lay quietly waiting.

Suddenly into that silence came a voice, old and cracked and creaky. It came up through the deck, up from below.

"Three fathoms down," it said. "Three fathoms down. I'm Davy Jones."

Chapter 14

An Old Friend

The voice taunted me, calling now from right below my feet, now from the foot of the mizzen. "I'm Davy Jones," it said again. Then came a rustling, scratching sound before it called again from behind me.

"Three fathoms down. Three fathoms more."

I whirled to face it, but stared only at an empty deck.

A screech, and an eerie, chattering laugh sounded. "Throw me a line, matey."

"Where are you?" I shouted. "*Who* are you?" My voice was swallowed by the trees and the thrum of distant surf. There was only the stillness for an answer.

The sharks circled round the brig. The dead men stood their horrid watch. And I felt drawn to that one voice, that one life in an empty world, for surely — whatever it was — it was alive.

The companionway was open, and I went down without a glance at the helmsman. I came into a ship that seemed to have been suddenly abandoned just hours before, yet oozed the desertion of an ancient ruin. In the captain's cabin, a pipe was set out on the table, atop an open pouch of tobacco, and by a candle sat a flint. In the galley I found plates arranged on the table with knives and forks beside them, a huge pot of stew grown cold and jellied on the stove. I could see where a man had sat whittling, there was a footprint in his shavings.

"I'm Davy Jones!" the voice screeched, shocking me with its suddenness. The scratching and rustling came from up forward, and then a banging of wood.

I went towards the voice with my heart in my mouth. I ducked under a hanging lamp and came into a cabin so dark that I could see nothing at first, and then only shapes. By the depth of their shadows, I knew that berths were stacked on either side, eighteen in all, in narrow tiers of three. I could tell that in four of them lay sailors, all still and silent. But the cabin pulsed with a steady little ticking noise, as though all of them had watches.

I was afraid of what I'd find, of what I'd feel if I went groping through the dark. So I fetched the candle from the captain's table, and brought its flame to light the cabin.

The sailors were covered by grey blankets that had been drawn up around their heads and shoulders. The

wool was thick with blood, and across the dark stains —
their legs ticking furiously — crawled thousands of
gleaming cockroaches.

Then, to my utter horror, one of the blankets fell to the
floor, shedding a mass of beetles. The sailor below it
heaved a leg over the side of his berth. He rose to his feet
and came staggering towards me.

His forehead was split right across, laid open to the
bone by a cutlass. His skin hung over his eyes like a
blindfold, dried to a hardness by clots of black blood. He
reached out his arms, and I moved back as he lumbered
down between the berths.

"Mate!" he cried. "Are you my mate?"

"No," I said, and he cowered back, his mouth in an
awful grimace of fear.

"Then you're one of *them*," he said.

"One of who?"

"Of them!" He tumbled forward, facedown on the
deck. The cockroaches swarmed over him in a sleek, black
carpet.

My candle went out. I turned and ran from the cabin,
slamming my head on the lamp, crashing into the table
with a rattle of dishes. I spun away from there, up to the
deck and the sunlight, to the crucified man, who grinned
at me with a leer that was all teeth and no lips.

I lay at his feet, on bleached planks warmed by the
sun. And soon I heard the most welcome, the most
wonderful sounds I had ever heard: a flapping of canvas;

a ripple of water; the splash of an anchor going down. I got to my knees and saw first the square topsail of a schooner, then a black hull below it, then the name *Apostle* and the numbers *1219* scrawled across the side.

Her decks were packed with men, and she anchored so closely that I could see the faces of those who tended the cable. Black and blond, bearded and not, they seemed the cruellest lot who had ever sailed a ship. In rags and bright bandanas, bedecked in glittering gold, they snubbed the cable and brought the ship to a stop beside me, under the dead gaze of the man they had crucified.

I retreated to the companionway. In the shelter of its hood, I listened as boats were lowered and oars fitted into pins. Then, fearing that the buccaneers would return to the brig, I crept below to find myself a weapon.

That awful laughter greeted me, and that voice came from everywhere. "I'm Davy Jones. Throw me a line, matey."

I sorted through the galley lockers, through drawers and shelves and bins. But the best I could find was a short, thick knife with a dull and rusted blade. Then I stood at the stove, digging clotted stew from the pot with my fingers, waiting for footsteps on the deck.

I resolved to fight until the end as bravely as I could, and hoped I might fall in a swift melee. I might take one or two of them with me, I thought, but I would not give myself up, no matter how they begged; I would not suffer the same terrible ends as my new shipmates.

But soon I grew teary-eyed at the thoughts of the coming battle. The stew sickened me until I could no longer eat; my hands and my legs trembled badly. I had to admit that I was scared — a coward at heart, I thought. And when I heard the boats going past in a chorus of rough voices and a splash of oars, I was more than immensely relieved.

I went to the stern cabin and, keeping myself to the shallows, peered out through the windows.

The brig had swung very close to shore. A thick mooring line drooped down from her stern, snaked through the water, and climbed again towards the trees. From the ship to the shore was a distance of less than fifty feet, but I thought of the sharks I had seen, and knew I'd never dare lower myself into that water.

The boats appeared below me, packed with men. Two passed side by side, then a third, and a fourth behind it. At a rough count there were sixty buccaneers, some in rags and some in finery, some with cutlasses and pistols, but most with no more weapons than I. They rowed towards a coconut grove, a crescent of golden sand.

Emboldened, I stood closer to the windows. The brig was drifting on the current, stretching out her mooring line as she swung across the bay. The cable lifted from the water, doubling my distance from the shore. But now I directly faced the coconut grove, and a crude sort of camp emerged from among the trees. There was a structure of logs, a firepit, a water barrel standing upright. And high on the sand lay a pair of ship's boats, once the complement — I thought — of my ill-fated brig.

The buccaneers spilled ashore, splashing through the shallows. With laughter and shouting and much hallooing, they swept up in a mass, and disappeared into the trees.

They left the beach deserted, their boats tethered to the coconut palms. Above me, the mooring line stretched as tight as a bar, and I thought that if I could pull myself along it, I might be able to reach the boats unseen and...

I groaned. The tide was flooding now. I had barely rowed against the current in the *Dragon*'s little dory; I could never hope to do it in a longboat built for twenty men. I would have to wait for the ebb again, nearly six hours distant. But at least I would have darkness on my side.

"Three fathoms down!" the voice cried suddenly. 'Throw me a line, matey."

I looked towards the sound, through the cabin door and up to the galley. I thought of the man I'd left lying on the deck in a swarm of cockroaches, and I imagined the voice was his, and that even now he was crawling aft. I could almost see him in the shadows, his eyes blinded by his own skin, his hands dark with blood, the mass of beetles ticking, ticking on his back.

I couldn't wait six hours. I couldn't wait another six *minutes* in the creaking old ship full of nightmares. I threw myself at the windows and fumbled with the latches. Just as I worked them open, another boat appeared below me.

It slid out from the curve of the old brig's hull, a boat smaller than the others, with only a few men instead of a pack. They were armed to the teeth with pistols and muskets and gleaming cutlasses.

The first oarsman passed, and then the second, dressed like the crew of an admiral's barge, in stripes of white and blue, in straw hats ribboned at the crowns. They bent forward, bent back, in perfect rhythm, and their feathered oars made hardly a ripple. I stood frozen at the windows; they needed only look up to see me.

Next came a figure in blue, standing upright with a cutlass for a cane, his hands folded on its guard. By the gold on his sleeve, by the bright plume in his hat, I knew it was Bartholomew Grace. He wore high boots curled down at the tops, and his wild, black hair covered his shoulders completely. He lifted his face towards the stretched-out mooring line, and I caught a glimpse — below the broad brim of his hat — of a smooth and pinkish cheek.

I was afraid that he would *feel* me watching him, yet I couldn't move away. My arms ached from the effort of holding them still, and my fingers started trembling so badly that the window latch rattled.

The oarsmen rowed swiftly, steadily, carrying that frightful figure along. But a man shouted at them from the stern, "Put your backs to it! Row, ladies, row!" He laughed, and I felt a great stir in my heart, for that laughter was so familiar.

He came into my sight an instant later, rocking back as the oarsmen pulled on their oars, as the boat lifted up at the bow. And it was true, though I could scarcely believe it. There, in his old crimson coat, with pistols stuffed all over him, sat Dashing Tommy Dusker.

I had known him as Dasher, and had seen him last on a forest road in Kent nearly eight months before. A highwayman, a smuggler, a rogue in a devilish way, he had been my shipmate on my first voyage in the *Dragon*. He'd been so scared of the sea that he had dressed himself in a suit of corks. That jerkin was gone now, but in its place he wore wineskins puffed with air, two of them slung over his neck and under his arms.

"Oh, you're doing fine, ladies, fine," he said. His hand on the tiller. "You can smell the gold now, can't you? Well, sniff at it, you dogs." He gave the rudder a little shimmy that made the boat rock side to side. Bartholomew Grace tipped sideways, leaning on his cutlass for support. And Dasher shouted, as though the bowman had done it, "Mind your oar there, Miller! I should slice a new one from your wooden head."

He seemed the same as ever, full of himself and as blustery as a north wind. How he had come to be part of a pirate crew was a mystery that I could not hope to solve, but I was desperately glad to see him. Dasher once had saved my life, and I felt now a desperate hope that he might somehow help me again.

In moments the boat grounded on the sand. The rowers held up their oars like four little trees, and Bartholomew Grace stepped between them, up the length of the boat, and onto the sparkling sand. With its silver at his feet and the green of the island behind him, in his blue and gold and crimson, he looked the very picture of a pirate, the way an artist might have thought a pirate *ought* to look. He stood with his back to me, and the breeze ruffled at his sweeping plume, at the ribbons in his rowers' hats, and then he strode up to the camp with his black boots shining, towards the shouting and laughter that fell to silence at his coming.

I waited until his boat had emptied, and at last I moved from the window. I threw myself down on the captain's settee, hoping to sleep until nightfall. But all manner of schemes ran through my mind, each seeming brilliant at first, all dissolving into hopelessness.

I wondered where the *Dragon* was; surely she waited for me *somewhere*. I closed my eyes and tried to picture the island as I had seen it on the chart; I got up again to rummage through the captain's desk for a pen and paper. And I sketched it there: the island; the rocks; the narrow little spit at the north of the harbour; and the beaches beyond it, where even now my little ship might be lying on the beach, her repairs under way. Yet just as easily, she might be standing off to the south or anchored at a cay, and I drew arrows and anchors all over my map before it occurred to me that the *Dragon* might even be off on her way to England.

In the end, it came down to one choice: I had to get away from the island. I had to take a boat that would let me search for the *Dragon*. If I couldn't find her, I had to sail to the next island, and the next, and on and on, if need be, until I found someone, somewhere, who would take me home to England.

I kept getting up and going back to the windows, staring out at the boats on the beach. But right beyond them were the buccaneers, busy with some sort of labour that took them in and out of the camp. If I was somehow going to steal a boat, it would have to be done right beneath their noses.

Finally, I did sleep. When I woke, it was dark.

A huge fire roared and cracked at the pirate camp. Its flames soared up through the coconut palms and I saw the buccaneers in their ragged clothes, turned orange by the light, then dark as demons as they passed before the fire. They carried chests and bags down to the beach, to a pair of boats that shuttled back and forth under bright, guttering torches. The harbour was ablaze with firelight.

And somewhere in my haunted ship came that rustling sound. And that cracked and broken voice cried out, "I'm Davy Jones. Three fathoms down!"

The sound was louder than I'd ever heard it, and through the darkness of the brig, this thing came scratching, screeching, ticking towards me.

"*Show no quarter!*" it screamed.

Chapter 15

Crawling with Cannibals

The door to the cabin creaked as something pushed against it. I squinted into layers of shadows that shifted in the fiery glow from the windows. I could see nothing but could imagine anything, and in the dark mass that moved along close to the deck, I formed the shoulders and the battered head of the man I had left covered in cockroaches. I saw his arm stretch out, his fingers spread. Then he leapt from the deck.

He hurtled towards me and crashed against my shoulder. I fended him off, feeling a hardness first and a softness below it, as though my hand had passed through a mass of beetles. And he tumbled back with a deathly shriek, only to swoop up again and batter at my face and arms. Then he shot past crashing against the windows with a jarring bang of wood and glass. And I saw him there, silhouetted in the flames of the buccaneers' fire.

It was only a parrot, old and tattered, as bedraggled as a bunch of dead flowers. "I'm Davy Jones," he said, and squawked. "Three fathoms down. Three fathoms more."

With his beak and his claws, he bashed at the window frame.

The noise he made seemed shockingly loud. "Stop that!" I hissed, but he went at it all the harder. He scratched and banged, and the noise came back in echoes, doubled by the trees, trebled by the hills. In the middle of the harbour, the torches of a passing boat shifted into line as the rowers turned towards me.

I cowered down below the windows and watched the light play across the overhead in watery patterns of yellow and gold. The parrot banged and clattered; the light grew brighter, filling the cabin. I glanced up to see a face at the window.

Under a black and tattered beard, it was gaunt and yellowed by fever and the torchlight. The skin was sunken so tight on the bones that it looked like a bearded skeleton grinning in towards me, and I gasped.

The parrot leapt up at the glass. The latch sprang open, the window swung out, and the bird vanished through it in a rush of feathers. The face fell away, followed instantly by a great thump and a roar of oaths. Then the parrot shrieked, "Hoist the colours!" — and I saw him perched on the mooring line that was again stretched taut by the night-time ebb. He was twitching his head like a man with the fits.

From the boat rose a howl of coarse laughter. "It's the parrot," said a voice... gruff as a bear's. "It's Dasher's blasted parrot."

But another, softer, said, "There's someone in there, I tell you. I saw him myself."

Again the buccaneers laughed. The fumes of their torches came in through the window, and their light flamed all across the glass. And the skeleton said, "Row me up to the chains. I'm going aboard for a look."

"Ghosts is all you'll find," said the gruff voice. But oars thumped against the hull as the boat made its way forward. The torchlight slipped across the windows, darkened, and fell away.

I looked out through the windows, straight towards the huge flare of the buccaneers' fire. It cast bright, flickering patches onto the calm of the harbour. The lights from the boat were smaller streaks of yellow that came down the length of the brig and lay like cords of gold below me.

I pushed the window wide and clambered onto the sill. Even reaching up, I couldn't quite touch the mooring line. But the parrot, with an angry squawk, reached down and pecked my hand.

"Go on!" I said, a soft shout through gritted teeth. "Get out of there." I shooed him off.

He hopped sideways down the line, turning himself

end for end. I crouched on the narrow sill, my hands on the frame at either side. Half a ship length away, a boathook caught onto the chains with a little clang of metal, and I leapt from the sill.

The line scraped across my arms and nearly pulled through my fingers. But I caught it, swinging in the air as the parrot screamed and chattered. He hopped away again, going towards the shore along the line in a funny, sidling walk.

Very clearly, I heard the footsteps on the deck. But the rail was above me, and all I saw, black against the stars, was the poor, dead watchman on the mainyard.

The window hung open at the stern of the ship, a sure sign, I thought, that I had passed through it. So I reached out with my feet, swinging madly from the line as I kicked it shut. Firelight glared off the glass, for a moment filling the cabin. And I saw my map on the captain's table, my sketch with its scribbles and notes.

The footsteps grew louder. I looked up at the rail, sure that I would see the buccaneer grinning at me. But then my mind, tortured by worries, thought of the helmsman what if the footsteps were his? I imagined him pulling his hands free from the nails, staggering across the deck. And what if the face that I saw was his: that grin without lips; those cold, dead eyes; his corpse's hands reaching out?

It filled me with such a terror that before I knew it I'd swung up my legs and caught the line in my knees. I scuttled along it as fast as I could, hanging upside down like a sloth. The parrot went before me, facing east and then west, tilting onto each leg in turn, all the time uttering strange little warbles, as though he thought it tremendous fun.

I was halfway to shore when my back touched the sea.

From my own weight, or from some shift in the currents, the brig had swung closer to shore, and the line sagged in the middle. Soon my shoulders were wet, and then my trousers, and I was pulling myself through the water.

And out of the bright reflections of fire came the fin of an enormous shark.

It sliced through the patterns of yellow and red and tore them to tatters, a black sickle racing across the harbour. The shore was only yards away. I could see Dasher very plainly, standing by the barrel. I pulled frantically at the line. But the shark came faster.

It butted my legs and tore me from the line. It whirled me deep in the sea, turned, and came at me again.

I hadn't the strength to fight it; I barely had the will. I sank until my face was underwater, and then a calmness came over me. I felt as though I floated in the sky instead of the sea, high above the little harbour with its blazing yellow lights. And the deeper I sank, the higher I floated, until the whole island was somehow laid below me.

Then my chest rested on the sagging loop of line, and I could go no deeper. Without thinking, I held on to it, and it seemed to anchor me high in the heavens. I felt the brig tugging at the end; the line tightened across my chest. As the brig swung out on the current, the line lifted me from the water just as the shark came back to the surface. I saw its teeth and the dark gleam of an eye. Then it passed below me, so close that the fin ripped across my leg.

The parrot was gone. Half drowned, nearly mad with fright, I felt a pity for it that was far beyond what I should have felt. I *cried* for the parrot as I pulled myself along the line, from the water to the shore. Then I let my legs swing down and fell on top of them, in a heap on the warm, hard sand.

It seemed that hours had passed since I'd leapt from the window of the anchored brig. But the buccaneers' boat still lay at its side, and the man with the torch was only then coming up from below. He carried his light through the companionway, and the crucified helmsman was outlined for a moment before him, arms spread wide, as though the dead embraced the living. Then the torch went quickly up the deck, its light flickering in the rigging.

He would have found my map, I thought. He would have found the unlatched window, the wood all scarred by the parrot's claws. Soon a search would start, and they'd find me quick enough, for the first place they'd look would be where the line came to shore.

I got up and moved shakily into the trees. The jungle was so thick that it soon swallowed me up, and by the time I'd gone a dozen paces I no longer knew where the water was. From the ship, the island had seemed deadly quiet, but here it breathed with animal sounds, with rustlings and tickings and strange little cries. Into my head rushed my boyhood fears of the forest, and my father's warning that the Caribbean crawled with cannibals. *They cook you alive, or so I've heard. They boil the flesh off you, then shrink your head to the size of a walnut.* And suddenly those imagined cannibals were all around me, creeping closer; the rustling was their bare feet in the forest, the ticking was the sound of poisoned arrows being nocked into bowstrings. I imagined myself being carried off by tattooed men with bones in their lips, men I'd never see until their hands reached out to grab me.

I turned at every noise. I jumped at every snapping twig. Soon I feared the cannibals that *weren't* there more than the pirates that were. The great, hot fire was like a beacon, and it drew me to its edge, where the light was dim enough to hide me yet bright enough to chase the shadows from the jungle close around.

I crept from tree to tree, circling the pirate camp, making for the west, where I thought I'd find the *Dragon*. At the deepest point of the circle, I looked up to see Dasher in the firelight. He stood not more than a dozen feet away, with his back towards me as he leaned against a barrel. He'd taken the air from his wineskins, and they hung flat against his sides. A little trickle of water, fed from a crude wooden trough, fell into the barrel, overflowing from the top and leaking through the staves.

Beyond Dasher and the barrel, in stacks round the fire, were silver ingots and bars of gold, boxes and chests of every size. I saw a tangled pile of shovels and picks, and guessed that all I saw had been unearthed from the island and brought here for loading aboard the *Apostle*. Even as I watched, the work continued, as men tramped from the beach to carry off another load. In the crew of nearly a hundred men, only two seemed idle. Bartholomew Grace, standing high on an iron-strapped chest, watched in all his finery. He looked like a prince or a king, his cutlass tipped on the chest, his hand on the hilt with his gold-braided cuff swaying in slow circles.

The other man was Dasher. He never moved from the barrel, never moved at all except to dip water for others with a ladle that was tied to his wrist. It seemed he guarded the barrel as though the water were more precious than all the silver and gold.

I thought of calling to him, but the idea passed as a fancy. Whatever he was when I'd known him before, he was a pirate now, and I had to find him alone if I hoped for him to help me. Dasher was kindly at heart, but among rogues he was a rogue himself.

I crept on, circling behind him. But I kept an eye on the buccaneers, and didn't see the dead branch in my path until it broke under my foot with a loud and shocking crack.

And Bartholomew Grace shouted out, "Stop where you are!"

Chapter 16

Gone Aground

"Do you think I'm blind?" roared Bartholomew Grace. "Do you think I don't have eyes in my head?"

He stepped down from his chest, and the firelight glittered on all his gold. For a moment it reached his face below the broad brim of his hat, and it seemed to me again that he *had* no face.

I crouched like a runner, ready to flee. I would take my chances with the cannibals and the jungle before I gave myself up to a gang of buccaneers.

But Grace turned away, and his black hair hid the pink smoothness of his cheeks. "Miller!" he shouted. "Come here."

Into the firelight stepped the rower that Dasher had

cursed. In his striped jersey and straw hat, he looked like a frightened boy. He trembled as Grace took a step forward.

The cutlass flashed fire, and the tip sliced through the seaman's jersey. A long, red bundle came tumbling out, and the sailor clutched at it, groaning. I thought the man's innards had been torn from his body, but then coins fell out, sparkling guineas that spilled to the ground, and I saw that the redness was no more than a length of fine silk.

"You're a thief," said Grace. "What do you have to say for yourself?"

The man stared wretchedly down at the silk and the coins.

"Speak, I tell you." But the man didn't answer, and I had never seen such a silent group as that crowd of buccaneers.

"By the Black Book and the laws of Oleron," said Grace, judge and jury too, "a thief shall pay for his crimes". He kicked through the silk and coins. "What have you got there? Ten guineas — a dozen, perhaps?" Then he shouted out, "What's an arm worth, bosun? What does the code say an arm is worth?"

"Ten guineas, sir," said a voice from the crowd.

Grace nodded, the red plume tossing on his hat. "Take him off." He motioned with the cutlass. "Exact his payment."

Miller was led away, and a moment later I heard a

blow of an axe and a shriek that rose and filled the island, a ghastly and terrible cry.

"Good Lord," said Dasher softly.

"Is there anyone else?" asked Grace, his voice as soft as rain. He walked through the group with long and graceful strides, wheeling left and then right. "Are there any more thieves among us? Anyone else who's turned against me?"

The buccaneers shifted around him. I could feel their terror, their dread of the man. One started keening, swaying on his feet with a pitiful moan. Grace silenced him with a swift slash that opened the fellow's cheek in a bright red smear. Another shouted, "Long live Captain Grace!" The cry was taken from man to man, though there was not a sailor in the lot who met the captain eye to eye.

In moments he'd exposed two more thieves. Their treasures seemed paltry and dismal, mere handfuls amid a hoard of gold. But one of the men paid for his crime with an eye, and his agonised screams stretched my nerves so far that I feared they would snap. The other thief threw himself at the pirate's feet, grovelling on the ground atop the sad little pile of Miller's coins and cloth.

"Ah, remorse," said Grace. "It calls for mercy, such a show as this. Stand up, man." He poked his cutlass down, and seemed to pry the fellow from the ground. "How much have you got there?"

The man held out his hands. I couldn't see what was

in them, but Grace bent his head and sifted through it with his fingers. "Thirty guineas," he said, and clucked his tongue. "Have you anything to say for yourself?"

The man was weeping. He tried to speak, but only a grunt came out. "Water," he said.

"Water?" Grace nodded. "Aye, we'll give you water, and see if that loosens your tongue." He stepped back. "Put him in the barrel."

To my amazement, Dasher laughed. It was a loonish cackle. "In the barrel?" he said. "Is that the best you can do? Make a pickle of him? And you call yourself a buccaneer?"

Every head swivelled towards him. Every face glowed from the fire. I sank down into the undergrowth, but I couldn't take my eyes from Bartholomew Grace. His face was flat and twisted, as though *melted* to his bones.

"In Kent that's a boy's game," said Dasher. "Every Sunday we put a parson in a barrel and make him spout his prayers." He stepped backwards, towards me, away from the barrel. "You've got a thirsty cove, you set him on a fire. You toast him, mateys; that's justice. That's what I say..."

His voice trailed off. Every man stared at him, but none with such wonder as the poor soul with this thirty-guinea debt.

Bartholomew Grace put the point of his cutlass on the ground. "Come here," he said, and beckoned to Dasher. "Come, come, my fine fellow."

I could see Dasher hesitate. But true to form, he stepped no closer to danger than he had to. "Toast him," he said, "if you've got the heart for it." He glanced back, as though judging the distance he would have to travel into the darkness. His face was pale and sweaty. "What say you, mateys? Toast him or drown him?"

The buccaneers were silent. Bartholomew Grace came walking between them, and I felt sick with the fear that Dasher would turn and bolt, that the pirates would follow, only to head straight towards me. I dared not move as Grace came closer to the barrel.

But only halfway there, he stopped as a voice shouted up from the water. A torch came flickering through the trees, and I sank deeper into the jungle.

The torch wove between the trees, shining onto fronds and ferns. And into the camp burst the gaunt and bearded man I'd seen at the windows of the brig. He held a piece of paper, which he flung to the ground at the captain's feet. "Look there!" he cried. "That come from the ship out there."

Grace picked up my map with his cutlass; he speared it with the point and held it up for all to see.

"There *was* someone on that ship," said the bearded man. "Now he's on the island."

Dasher didn't wait for orders. He pulled pistols from his bandolier and fired them wildly into the sky. "After him, mateys!" he shouted. "Follow me!" His long, red coat whirled around him as he turned and raced into the jungle.

He passed within a yard of me, hurdling branches, thrashing at ferns. He ran like a bull through the trees, and I jumped up and started after him, afraid that Grace and all the others would be coming on his heels.

I didn't look back, nor did Dasher. His long legs swept him along, crashing from tree to tree. His hat sailed off and fluttered past my shoulder. I heard voices behind me, but they soon faded away. Yet on we ran through the jungle and glade, over streams and under windfallen trees; we ran for half a mile or more until, at last, I caught up to him in a starlit clearing and clutched to the tails of his coat.

Dasher squealed. It was a pathetic sound, and he hurled himself down in a tight little ball, like a porcupine but with his pistols for quills. He covered his face with his hands, and a wineskin flattened under his shoulder with a tiny mouselike squeak.

"Dasher," I said, panting. "Dasher, it's John."

He spread his fingers apart and peered up at me in the darkness. "John Spencer?" he said.

"Yes," I told him.

"Well, knock me down with a feather." He sat up, and it cheered me to see his old rakish grin. "I'm surprised you could catch me, matey," he said. "There's horses that don't run as fast as Dashing Tommy Dusker."

"What are you doing here?" I asked.

"Treasure." He winked broadly. "Silver and gold, matey."

"Stop saying that," I snapped.

"I'm sorry," he said. "It's a habit. Join up with pirates and you talk like a pirate."

"You joined them?" I asked.

"John," said he, "I'm the king of all the pirates."

Months before, he had told me he was the king of all the smugglers, but he'd been nothing more than a laughing stock by day, and by night, a highwayman who never made much success of robbing coaches.

He collected the pistols that had tumbled from his belt and stuffed them back in place. "That Bartholomew Grace, he fairly hops at my words. Oh, he lives in dread of Tommy Dusker, let me tell you."

"Indeed," I said drily "I saw that."

"Did you?" he asked. "The barrel?"

I nodded.

"You know what was in there?"

"Water," I said.

He laughed. "Silver, matey. And gold. Pieces of eight and louis d'or and more doubloons than you've got hairs on your head." He stood up and tugged at his wineskins. "If they'd put that pirate cove into the barrel, they wouldn't have got his ears wet before they squashed him against the treasure I hid in there. And then Grace would have tallied it up, and started counting my arms and my legs, and there wouldn't have been much of me left when he'd taken his payment. Just a head and guts, that's all I'd be. Just a poor blind head you could carry about in a basket."

"And to save yourself, you would have thrown that man on the fire?"

"Oh, they wouldn't have done it," said Dasher. "Not Grace. He's scared of fire, John. Scared to death of fire. Did you see his face? It's burned away like a candle stub. You'd go stark raving mad to look at that face in the daylight."

We started walking, away from the prick of light, faint as a fallen star, that was all we could see of the buccaneers' fire. No one had come very far after us, but I saw little comfort in that. There was nowhere we could go; and at daylight they would hunt us down.

We stumbled onto a path that was so dark and walled by growth that it might have been drilled through the jungle. And we followed it up the hillside by feel alone, brushing ferns with either hand. It had been only recently made, but already the jungle was narrowing its sides, closing it in like a scar. I wanted to listen for cannibals, but Dasher — of course — talked all the time. He told me about the treasure — it was Kidd's, he said — and how he'd come to find it.

"Just after I saw you last — in Kent, remember — I went down to Sussex and met a codger there, an old Jack nastyface. A hundred years old if he was a day, all wrinkles and liver spots. But there he sat at the Black Horse Inn, singing songs and crying for the rum, so I stood him a glass, and he gave me a tale. Well, he sailed with Kidd, or so he said, and he knew where the treasure lay. 'Where?' I say, and the codger, he needs another glass. He has an old parrot on his shoulder that's tottering on its legs; the parrot's drinking too, drink for drink from the same glass. And the codger says, 'The parrot knows.' It was Kidd's parrot, he says; his name is—"

"Davy Jones!" I cried.

Dasher stopped in midstep. "You've seen him?" he asked.

"I was aboard the brig," I said.

"That blasted parrot." Dasher tugged at his wineskin. "He hates me, John. For bringing him back here, I think."

"But how did you get here?" I said.

"Aren't I tellling you, John?" Dasher walked away, and I hurried after him. "'The parrot knows,' says the old codger. He says he'll give me the parrot for a bottle of rum. 'Good rum, mind,' he says. Then he sits there, all stony-faced, until the bottle's standing beside him. 'Culebra,' he says. 'Take the parrot to Culebra,' and he starts in on his rum. Well, it's the last bottle he'd ever have in this world, for by morning he was dead, stretched out on the floor, bung upwards, as stiff as a plank. And that old parrot was perched on his nose, railing away like a devil. Took me days to get him sober again."

"The sailor?" I asked. "I thought he was dead."

"No, the parrot!" laughed Dasher. "He was drunk as a lord."

"And then what?" I asked.

"Word got round that there was a fellow who knew all about Kidd's treasure."

"How?" I said.

"Well, I let it out myself. In every inn from Eastbourne round to Romney, I told the keeper that a handsome lad, a dashing cove up by Alkham, knew exactly where it was. And they beat a path to my door, John. Squires and lords and ne'er-do-wells, they came running for a shot at that gold. We put an outfit together and hired that brig you found in the harbour, and we sailed her all the way from Bristol. Clear across the sea."

There was a shiver in his voice as he talked of that; I could imagine the fear he'd felt to be in a world of water.

"True enough, the parrot knew where the treasure was. I tied him to a string, and he whirred round my head. Then off he went like a shot, flitting through the jungle, squawking like a fishwife, up to the breast of this hill."

Just as he said it, we came out of the jungle, onto a flat shoulder of land with little dunes in an arc on its far side. Stars shone above us, and the pale lines of surf were laid out like bones on the black of the eastern sea. Then Dasher stopped, and as I came up beside him he put out an arm and stopped me too.

We stood at the edge of a deep, cavernous pit. Nearly fifty feet from top to bottom, bordered by the heaps of dirt I'd thought were dunes, it smelled of the earth and of mouldering wood. And it reeked of gunpowder.

"This is where the parrot came," said Dasher. "He started hopping about, yelling, 'Three fathoms down! Three fathoms more!' We started digging, and nine feet

150

deep we came to a platform of coconut logs. The bloody parrot, we thought; he can't count. But we hauled the logs out and kept on going, and we found another platform three feet farther, and a third at fifteen feet. Then the treasure, John. Lord almighty, the treasure! We broke open the first layer and we swam in the guineas and jewels. We drowned ourselves in the treasure, John. Only when we came out, Bartholomew Grace was standing right where you are now."

Dasher shook himself. The night breeze purred through the jungle canopy, and I heard the hushed pulsing of the surf.

"He'd been on the island all the time, with that black ship of his anchored on the eastern shore, and you can't see that from here. He was scratching for treasure along the beaches, just sticking a shovel in wherever he pleased; he'd been at it for years, I think, off and on."

So Horn had been right. I cursed myself for siding with Abbey instead.

"I was down in the hole," said Dasher, pointing at the pit. "Grace was up here, and oh, he cut a fine figure in his gold and his feathers, the wind at the tails of his coat. And that face of his glaring down — I thought it was Death himself standing above me."

We sat at the edge of the pit, our backs to the jungle. I kept looking behind me, to the left and the right, but Dasher kept his head down, staring into that hole.

"He killed us all, John. Every man on the ship, every

man in the pit. You poke about in that dirt there, you'll find their bodies fast enough. There's not more than a scraping on top of them. John, it was awful. I don't like to think of the things he did."

"But he spared you," I said.

"Well, I joined up with them, John. I told you that. 'Hold on!' I said. 'I'm Dashing Tommy Dusker.' Oh, I talked a blue streak, and they saved me in the end, because I joined up with them."

"I would never do that," I said.

"Better a pirate than a corpse — my mother's own words. And I thought I'd be rid of them soon enough, until we got down to the harbour and I saw what they'd done to the watch on the ship. Men nailed to their posts, the sharks in a frenzy. 'You're in a fix now,' I told myself. 'You've come out of the pan and into the fire, you have.'"

Dasher kicked his heels at the edge of the pit. "That very day we set to work carrying the treasure down, and there was no one carried it faster than Tommy Dusker. I'm strong as an ox, you know that."

I nodded; he was easy to please.

"There were forty kegs of powder buried here, and cases of arms, but I only carried treasure. Every trip I made, I stopped at the barrel and had a drink, dropping in a little something for myself: a pocketful of jewels, a few doubloons, those blasted Froggy coins. I filled that barrel until there was just enough room for the ladle. Then off we went to bring the ship round, and what do we see but the *Dragon* standing off the harbour."

He grinned and shook his hair. "You came after me, didn't you, John? You heard the stories, and thought you'd throw in your lot with Dasher again. Oh, all of London must be abuzz about me now."

That was all he'd ever wanted, to be famous for his deeds. I hadn't the heart to tell him that he'd been the farthest thing from my mind. With my silence I let him believe what he wanted.

"So where is she?" he asked. "Where's the *Dragon* now?"

I shrugged.

"You don't know?"

"No," I said. I told him how I'd come to be on the island, starting with my dory ride and ending with my last sight of the *Dragon* sailing round the point.

"No matter," said Dasher when I'd finished. "She won't have gone far, and we'll see her at daybreak. Grace will clear off on the evening tide, and we can slip in and get my barrel. It's not as much as it might have been, but still it's a fortune, John. A handsome little fortune."

"Bartholomew Grace will take it," I said.

"He won't," said Dasher. "It's just a leaky old barrel to him."

His confidence raised my spirits slightly, and we sat to wait for dawn. It came swiftly, as it always does in the tropics, and we watched the sun rise from an endless ocean. The tide was low and rising, and I saw every reef and rock and cay painted white with surf. But the *Dragon* wasn't there.

To the south, the harbour was open below us. The *Apostle* and the brig lay side by side, and the buccaneers' boats were like little toys rowing to and fro. But we didn't watch for long; we went down the northern face of our hill, and crossed the island to the western shore.

We came to a huge, flat sandy beach, and the bright blue of the Caribbean sea. A mile off, or a little more, was the humped island of Luis Peña Cay. And above its trees, thin as sticks, poked the masts of the *Dragon*. They were slanted far to the side, and the topsail yard made them look like a fallen cross.

"Good Lord," said Dasher. "They've gone aground. They've wrecked themselves out there."

Chapter 17

A Strange Ambition

"They're not wrecked," I said. "They've careened the ship." But in my heart I feared he was right. Either way it made little difference, for we couldn't hope to reach the cay without a boat. No matter how I looked at it, we were stranded on the island.

"We'll have to wait," said Dasher.

"Can you go back and get a boat?" I asked.

"From Bartholomew Grace? Not a chance!"

"Why not?" said I. "You told me you've joined them."

"Well, it was just a temporary join," he said. "A bit of paste is all, not a mortice and tenon. If I showed my face at the pirate camp, they'd slice me up like a carrot."

"Then what do we do?" I asked.

"We wait, like I said." And with that Dasher sat on the sand, his back against a coconut palm. "The tide's flooding now. When it turns to the ebb, Bartholomew Grace will weigh anchor for Kingston."

"Why Kingston?" I wondered.

"Oh, he's got a plan," said Dasher. "He's got a lunatic scheme. He's going to stuff our brig with all the powder that he found, with the grenades and the bombs and all, and he's going to set it off in the middle of the English fleet. He's going to blow them all to kingdom come."

My head reeled at the thought. I remembered the ships in their tight columns and rows, and I saw a fire raging through them, leaping from mast to mast, from ship to ship. Each one was full of powder; each would explode in turn, spreading the flames farther and farther.

The fragile treaty that England had with France wouldn't last for very long. With her Indies fleet destroyed, England would be weakened everywhere. The peace was so tenuous that Grace might even break it by himself.

"He could start another war like that," I said.

"Why, that's just what he wants," said Dasher. "When a country's fighting, it doesn't bother much with buccaneers."

I prodded his shoulder. "Get up," I said.

Dasher tipped back his head. "Where are we going?"

"Back to the harbour." I pulled on the strap of his wineskin. "We have to sink that brig."

"Not I. No, thank you, John." He lowered his head to stare again across the sand, at the groundswell breaking in a steady heave of gold-stained water. "I'll stay here, I think. If what you say is right, and the *Dragon*'s just careened, she'll float up on the tide and we can signal to her then."

"The *Apostle* will be out," I said.

"But she won't. John, you don't think things through, that's your trouble. You're too quick to act, and you always were. Grace can't go out when the tide's on the flood."

He was right. I'd seen the way the current made a gate of the harbour entrance. It wouldn't open for Grace until the tide had peaked and was falling again. By then the *Dragon* would be floating.

Or would she?

"What if they careen the *Dragon* on the other side?" I said. "What if she really is wrecked?"

Dasher shrugged. "You pays your money, you takes your choice," he said in his cavalier way. "Maybe Grace gets out. Maybe he doesn't."

"Then he won't," I said. "I'll stop him myself if I have to."

"Which you will," said Dasher.

"All the glory will be mine," I added — rather slyly, I thought.

"And the bloodshed too, I should think."

Dasher wriggled down into the sand. One by one, he took the pistols from his belt and bandolier, and arranged them in rows on the beach. He opened his coat, then closed his eyes and settled back on his elbows.

"You won't help me?" I said.

"Why should I? What has England ever done for me? Tell me that," he said. "All she's done is bleed me dry from the taxes and the tariffs. She's made me a smuggler and a highwayman and a pirate too, just to make an honest living. And some fine day she'll haul me off to Scraggem Fair and put a noose round my neck." He twisted his head violently, and gurgled in his throat. "The crowds will come that day, all the Mrs Hickenbothoms and the Mr Thingamabobs, and they'll cheer for me then, right enough. 'There he goes,' they'll say. 'The cove that stole Kidd's treasure.' Then the trapdoor will open, and they'll watch me come down with the hempen fever, and it will be the grandest hanging they've ever seen. *That's* how I'm going to die."

It was the strangest ambition I'd ever heard, though it wasn't the first time he'd told it to me. Poor Dasher wanted only to be famous, as much a rogue as Dick Turpin.

"You know what I'm going to do when I get home?" he asked. "I'm going to take all my silver and gold and buy myself a lordship. And a cauliflower for my head. Then I'll ride in from the highway and sit in the House of Lords with my coat and my guns, and make laws that are fair. 'You were caught smuggling tea, were you, lad? Well, good for you. What's that you say: pay duty? Why no, my fine fellow. You were only *doing* your duty.' What a pistol I'll be. What a swashbuckler!"

It was clear that he wouldn't help me. So I turned away and walked up the beach towards the narrow spit that I would cross to reach the harbour. The sand was hot and white and it squeaked below my boots; on my right the surf curled up and hammered at the beach.

I'd gone a dozen yards when Dasher shouted, "Wait!" When I looked back, he was up on his feet, stuffing his guns into place. He ran towards me, staggering as he slipped in the sand. A gun fell loose; he stooped and took it up. And he hurried along beside me.

"Do you think there's really glory in it?" he asked.

"I doubt it," I said.

"Surely there is. It's the sort of thing they write ballads about, isn't it? 'The English fleet he did save from the heat.'"

He stood breathing hard, his hair and his side-whiskers bright in the sun, a strange grin set crooked on his face. I could see that, for once, he wasn't thinking of himself. He was frightened — for me. That thought scared me more than anything else.

"Let's go," he said.

We walked side by side up the beach, his big coat flapping at his legs. We made one shadow on the sand, like a two-headed eagle. Then we slipped through the gap and crouched in the undergrowth at the edge of the harbour.

The buccaneers still laboured with the treasure. Their boats shuttled back and forth, from shore to ship, carrying treasure onto the schooner and powder onto the brig. The crucified corpse stood his never-ending trick at the wheel, but the dead watchmen were gone from the yard and the capstan. The sharks circled lazily as the brig swung with the currents on the tether of her mooring line. She was deeper in the water by a foot or more, a floating bomb full of powder. But the mooring line stretched stiff one moment and hung loose the next as the tide boiled into the harbour. I knew I couldn't get out there; I could never get aboard her.

The *Apostle* lay behind the brig, anchored fore and aft. The black hull was hidden from our view, and all the masts and yards seemed to belong to one enormous vessel.

In four hours, or a little more, the tide would be full. It would turn to the ebb, and Grace would sail his ships out towards Kingston. I saw no way to stop him, short of chaining the brig to the shore. And then I laughed, for the answer came to me right away, and it was so simple that I should have seen it sooner.

"We *can't* keep the brig where she is," I said. "It's impossible."

"I've been telling you that," said Dasher.

"But we *can* cut her loose."

He looked at me as though I'd gone feeble in the head. "John, she's anchored. She won't go very far."

"Far enough," said I, and Dasher frowned before he grinned.

"Why, they'll tangle like toms in a catfight," he said.

Suddenly he was keen to try. He led the way, in a wide circle behind the buccaneers' camp, then back towards the water. In high spirits again, he imagined the glory of saving the fleet.

"It's a lark," he said. "It's a grand scheme, right enough. We'll be famous, John. We'll get knighted, I wager. Sir Tommy Dusker. Sir *Thomas* Dusker. 'Aye, aye, Sir Thomas, whatever you say.' Just think, John; we might be written up in books someday."

"I'm *trying* to think," I said. "Once we've cut the line, what will happen then?"

"Why, we'll go to Buckingham Palace and kneel before the king," said Dasher. "He'll touch us with his sword, and say 'Arise, Sir Thomas.' He'll ask me how I got my fortune. 'To tell you the truth, I stole it,' I'll say. 'I'm a thief in the *knight*, Your Majesty.' And, oh, how the ladies will fancy me then."

He was too full of his dreams to think of *how* we would do it. I followed him through the jungle, his red coat moving before me like a dark hole that kept opening in my path. I decided we would cut the line and make our way back to the western beaches, and wait there for the *Dragon*. But the thought still nagged me: would the *Dragon* float again? What if half the crew had succumbed to the fever, and the rest — too weak to sail her — had driven the schooner ashore? Once we cut the line, our course would be set. At best we would gain only twelve hours, until the tide flooded again in the night and Bartholomew Grace sailed off for Kingston.

Dasher and I found the end of the mooring line turned twice around a coconut palm and seized at the bight in a cow hitch. We needed only to cut through that thin lashing to let the brig pull herself free.

Dasher took out his knife.

"Wait," I said.

The last of the boats were only then setting out from shore. In two of the three, pulling roughly at the oars, were ragged crews as much like apes as men. Sunlight sparkled on cutlasses and earrings, on the barrels of long muskets. But in the third came Grace, his straw-hatted, blue-ribboned men rowing like a racing crew, with one in rags in place of the wretch called Miller. The captain stood in the stern, one hand on the tiller, the other behind his back. With the glare on the surface, the golden sand below, he seemed to walk across the water. The sharks went with him, round and round his boat.

He would pass very close. I looked at Dasher and my heart gave a jump. In his red coat, with the sunlight filtering through the trees, he looked as bright as flames. If Bartholomew Grace so much as turned his head, he would surely see us there.

"Quiet," I said. "Not a sound."

The boats came on. We heard the thump and splash of oars, the chuckle of water at the bows. We heard the tiny flutter of the ribbons in the rowers' hats.

And with an awful screech, and a bloodcurdling yell, Davy Jones the parrot came hurtling through the jungle.

Chapter 18

Phantom Sailors

"Three fathoms down!" the parrot cried. "Three fathoms more." He came in gaudy flashes of yellow and red, low to the ground and high in the trees, then swooped with his thrashing wings and landed on Dasher's arm.

Dasher, startled, shouted out. "Get off!" he cried, shaking his arm. The parrot hopped up to his shoulder.

The boats turned towards us. The long guns lifted up to shoulders. Cutlasses gleamed like rows of sharks' teeth, razor sharp. In half a minute they'd be upon us.

"Run for it!" I said.

But Dasher pushed me down. He took one glance at me, then stood in his coat of flaming red. The parrot was pecking at his ear.

"Help yourself to my barrel," he whispered to me. "Good luck to you, John." Then he dropped his knife at my feet, and started down towards the water.

I wanted to run after him, but I couldn't. Dasher gave himself up so that I might stay hidden. And to my shame, I didn't move.

"It's only me," he shouted at the boats. "It's Dashing Tommy Dusker."

He went down to the shore, talking all the way. "I feared you'd maroon me," he said. "I went after that cove what came off the brig, and I hunted him down, mateys. I killed him, fair enough; I sliced his throat from ear to ear. Mateys, I done him in."

The straw-hatted rowers ground their boat ashore. Bartholomew Grace strode between them, then stepped up on the prow.

"Oh, Captain Grace, he was a wicked-fast runner," said Dasher. "I chased him clear across the island, but I ran him down in the treasure pit. So here I am, and if you think I've only been shirking my duty, then put me to work. Just give me a rope, Captain, and I'll pull it or tie it; whatever you please."

Grace looked at him for the longest time. Then Davy Jones hopped up to Dasher's head and started plucking at his hair.

"And see; I've got my parrot back," said Dasher with a strange laugh that nearly broke my heart. "Oh, mateys, isn't this grand?"

They took him off in the boat. I saw his red coat climbing up the side of the brig; then it was lost in the swirl of men. Only later would I learn what task Grace had in store for Dasher. But if I'd known it earlier, I wouldn't have let him go.

His knife had vanished in the undergrowth. I groped through the ferns, slowly at first and then frantically, until I found it trodden into the ground, and my hand closed around the blade. With some sadness, I saw that Dasher had blunted the tip.

His pistols, I knew, were never loaded with balls. They were packed with enough powder to make a great noise and a fine show of flames, but they were no more dangerous than firecrackers. For all his bluster and talk, Dasher was a harmless soul with a great dislike for suffering.

I took the thick rope in my hand, touched the blade to the lashings. Then I stopped, and stared down through the trees at the harbour.

What would happen to Dasher, I wondered, if I cut through the lashing? He had only just emerged from the jungle; surely, if the brig came free right then, the buccaneers would believe he had done it.

With a sigh, I resolved to wait. But I soon came to see that I could only gain by waiting; if the ships tangled when the tide was full, the buccaneers might be trapped for the next change of the tide as well. I had to admit that Dasher was right; I had acted too quickly, and my hurry had put him in danger.

I settled deep in the ferns and watched through a curtain of fronds as the buccaneers readied the brig for her voyage. They lashed the sails along the yards, first the courses, then the topsails. They let them hang in place, and the shadows of the workers were cast sharply on the canvas until a ghostly second crew seemed to emerge, writhing on the sun-bleached cloth that filled and emptied in the breeze. Giant phantom sailors — long-legged and black of skin — they rode within the sails, and their voices were the snap of rope, the crack of hardened canvas.

I watched them spin and leap to the drumbeat of the thudding sails, to the chanting of the buccaneers, and all the tales of cannibals that I'd ever heard filled my mind anew. I was like Robinson Crusoe, alone on my island, stricken with terror at the sight of dancing figures. I didn't know which was worse: to sit with my back to the dreaded jungle, or to turn away from the buccaneers. So I sat, all atremble, glancing again and again into the tangled growth around me. I had never felt so lonely, so full of a terrible pity for myself. I had been on the island for a little less than a day, but I ached to get off it.

As though to add to my misery, a fog came in from the sea. It covered the sun and blotted out the shadows on the sails. It touched the treetops, then crept among the bushes where I sat. Cold and clammy, it beaded water on every leaf and fern; it soaked me to the bone.

The ships grew faint and hazy; the voices of the

buccaneers seemed to come from the island instead of the ship. And through the jungle, in the fog, swirled mysterious shapes that, the harder I stared, looked more and more like savages. The drip of water, the rustling of ferns, sounded to me like bare feet padding slowly closer. Here a spike of ferns appeared to be the feathers in a cannibal's crown; there a knothole white with sap was a human eye turned towards me.

When I could bear it no longer, I took Dasher's knife and cut through the lashing. The brig turned slowly, and the mooring line uncoiled from the tree like a great white snake. It slithered through the ferns, twisting and sliding down towards the water. Then the breeze, or a shift in the currents, took hold of the brig, and the line leapt through the last of the bushes.

I heard a shout, an oath, and then a roar of startled voices. The brig swung through the fog with her sails spread like wings, her yards crawling with men. There was a groan of wood, a shriek, the startling twang of breaking rope. A yard gave way, spilling men who tumbled in grey shapes like swooping birds; I heard the splashes as they hit the water, their high, short screams as the sharks found them there. Then the brig came to a stop, her sails fluttering.

I hadn't thought out what would happen next. I squinted at half-hidden shapes, trying to see what damage I'd brought. A shiver went through me at the sound of oars coming through the fog.

They thumped and creaked; the rowers grunted. A voice said, "Watch it!" And a boat scraped against the sand nearby.

I judged that it was very close; I dared not move. To my left, my bearded, skeletal friend came tramping along the beach, bent forward as he dragged a line that stretched out from his shoulder. Behind him came another, walking backwards with the same line in his hands, hauling it along, his heels kicking into the sand. The rope vanished into swirls of mist as though the men were pulling at the fog itself, trying to clear it from the ships.

Whether this was the same line that I'd cut or a new one, I could not tell. But I was sure the men would tie it to the stoutest tree they could find — and take great care doing it — so that the brig might be warped free from her embrace with the *Apostle*. I kept silent and still as the pair went by, then moved down to the beach and followed their tracks in the sand.

After just a few paces I saw the boat at the water's edge. Still floating, the oars laid neatly in place, it seemed to be waiting for me. I ran to the bow and was surprised to find no anchor, no line, nothing at all to keep the boat where it was. I pushed; it slid off from the sand. I waded after it and heard a dribble of water.

The sound came from the trees. Startled, I looked up to see the larger of the two men with his back towards me, a dark little river spreading down through the sand. Idly, he turned towards me, buttoning his trousers.

My feet might have been stones, so heavy did they feel. They anchored me there, and the man came running forward.

He didn't shout, he *growled*. It was a wordless cry, a savage sound that was low and full of rage. He came leaping over the beach in his ragged clothes. The shock of it freed me. I pushed the boat and clambered in; I snatched up a heavy oar.

The man bounded after me, over the sand, into the water. I poled with the oar. The boat slid out to deep water, but the man lunged forward and clutched the bow. He levered himself up as the boat slewed sideways. I pushed with the oar, deeper and deeper, until I could only barely touch the bottom.

The man's head rose over the side, and I saw a bloodied bandage wrapped tightly round his face. It was the man Grace had slashed across the cheeks; the growls were the only sounds he could make.

His elbow hooked across the gunwale; his shoulders lifted up. And he began to heave himself aboard.

Chapter 19

In the Gunsights

He was a big, powerful man. His arms were as thick as my legs. He hauled himself up from the water with a dreadful gleam in his eyes.

I thrust the oar down to push off again, and was horrified to feel no bottom below me, nothing to push against. Then the oar twisted in my hands, shoved from below with enough force that I was nearly levered from the boat. At the bow, the buccaneer's eyes bulged out; the blood-stained cloth twisted on his face. And he vanished from the gunwale. He disappeared without a sound, snatched away in a sudden boiling of crimson water. A shark's fin rose in the fog, then sank again, and all that was left was the bandage.

I sat and rowed, sobbing with fear. I worked the boat along the shore, cringing at the noise my oars made as they banged and rumbled in the pins. Built to be rowed by four strong men, the boat was more than I could handle. But I bent to my task until my arms ached and my back seemed hot with fire.

The dark shapes of the tangled ships passed on my left, the jungle on my right. I found a current close to shore, and rested as it pulled me on. Then I met the flood at the harbour entrance, and waited for the tide to turn.

Shouting started onshore, and carried to the ships. It began with a man's name and ended with a volley of oaths back and forth across the harbour. For the buccaneers, it was a mystery; one of their crew and one of their boats had simply disappeared. I grinned at the thought of the confusion I'd caused, the fear I'd put in their hearts. Like all sailors, they'd be superstitious men. They would search through their blooded souls and conjure all manner of madness from the fog and the island and the corpses they'd left in their wake.

When at last the tide turned in my favour, the ships were still entangled, the men still shouting in confusion. I kept myself clear of the shore, and let the currents carry me over the bar. Then again I set the oars between the pins, and started rowing to the west.

My boat pitched in the swell. The ebb pulled me to the east, towards the open ocean, and I struggled against it, afraid that if I once lost sight of the land I would never find it again. I rowed mindlessly, mechanically, thinking of nothing but the bump and creak of the oars.

In an hour I'd gone only a hundred yards, but at last I'd cleared the island's southern point. The sandy beaches where I'd walked with Dasher stretched beside me, until the fog closed them in. The ebb that had held me back now carried me on, through swirls of fog that swept down from the slopes of the island.

I judged the direction to Luis Peña Cay, and pulled towards it. Soon the fog broke into the long bands and canyons that I'd seen from the *Dragon* on our outward journey. And I rowed along, through sun and shadow, until I felt I couldn't possibly lift the oars for another stroke. Wearied to the bone, I rested a moment — only a moment, I thought.

I woke without knowing I'd fallen asleep. The boat rocked like a cradle, wrapped tightly in fog. I had lost sight of the sun, and all direction. I had no idea how far I had drifted.

With a groan I took up the oars. I turned the bow towards the waves, then bent forward and dug in with the blades. I dragged them back, pushed them forward: I felt as though I'd rowed for ever, and still had years to go.

Little whirlpools spun behind me. Then the fog seemed to break; it dissolved, revealing a sail. A hull emerged below it, huge and black. At the bow was a figurehead: a dragon.

It was Horn who pulled me aboard, Horn who came down from the martingales, shouting, "Starboard! Starboard!" at the helmsman, to steer the ship towards me. He grabbed my collar and pulled me up; he plucked me from the boat and left it there to drift along. The oars slid from their pins; the little boat smacked against the schooner, dipped, and filled with water.

"We'd given you up," said Horn. "All of us had."

He hauled me up to the deck, then held me because I could not keep my feet. He walked me down towards the stern, and the captain ran to greet us.

"John!" he cried, his arms wrapping round my shoulders. "Oh, blessed be!"

Abbey came behind him, and the little gunner clapped me on the back. All three of the men were bugbitten, their arms and necks scratched and spotted. They took me below and filled me with hot, thick soup as they begged to hear my story, everything I'd seen.

But first I asked about the *Dragon*. "You were driven off," I said. "What happened then? Did they chase you? Is the cargo ruined? And Mudge; is he well?"

"No, no, and yes," said Uncle Stanley with a smile. "The *Apostle* sailed straight into the harbour, so we went no farther than the cay. We careened the ship, and Abbey found a bruised plank just below the waterline."

"Right where you told me to look," said the gunner. "I wish I'd listened, John."

"And the fever?" I asked.

"It ran its course," said Butterfield. "We were blessed with good water at Luis Peña Cay."

"But the mosquitoes!" cried Abbey. "They're big as sparrows there." He scratched his neck, and his fingers came off spotted with blood. "I've never seen the likes of it. Enormous big brutes."

"The devil with your mosquitoes," said Horn. "I want to hear from the boy."

Uncle Stanley filled my bowl again, and I told them — between spoonfuls — all that I'd done and all that I'd learned. The last word was barely out of my mouth when Butterfield said, "We'll sail for Kingston." He made a fist and rapped it on the table. "By George, that's what we'll do."

I looked down at my soup, at a bowl that seemed bottomless. It was no more empty than the moment when I'd started.

"How does that sound, John?" asked Butterfield. "We'll sound the alarm, and the navy will deal with those rascals."

"What if Grace goes the other way instead?" I asked. "Wouldn't the fleet be packed just as tightly at English Harbour?"

Butterfield looked at Horn, who nodded slowly.

"I'm sure that's true," said Horn. "But why would Grace go south? He doesn't know the *Dragon*'s here."

"Their line was cut," I said. "Their boat disappeared."

"Why, they'd have to be witches to guess it from that," said Horn.

I stared glumly at my soup. I didn't want to put voice to my real fears, lest somehow it made them come true. But Dasher knew where the *Dragon* was, and I wondered if he would keep the secret if things went badly for him. I hated myself for leaving him in the hands of Bartholomew Grace.

"What else can we do?" asked Butterfield.

I watched the soup slosh in my bowl as the *Dragon* sailed along. Heading north and east, she put another dozen yards of water between us and Culebra with every moment that passed.

"They're bottled up in there," I said. "They're trapped. The brig is full of powder, and if we started shooting at it, wouldn't they surrender? Wouldn't they *have* to surrender?"

No one spoke.

"They can't even bring their cannons to bear," said I.

The *Dragon's* hull creaked like an old chair. I felt the water passing, the distance to Culebra growing larger.

Abbey coughed. "Blast me, I like that," he said. "We can pound them to splinters. Knock the sticks down, and where are they then?" He fairly thirsted for a shot at the *Apostle*. "Dismast them, I say; *then* sail to Kingston."

"And they can't shoot back?" said Butterfield.

"No, sir," I said.

It took him a long, full minute to think. "There's the cargo," he said. "We have to think of that. It's our duty to carry it home. And there's the welfare of the men."

"Let's have a crack at them, sir," said Horn. "If Grace gets out, only the devil can stop him."

Butterfield licked his lips. He touched his thin hair. "Oh, very well," he said. "I hope it's the *proper* thing to do."

We turned the *Dragon* and eased the mainsail out. She rolled through the swell and ran steadily to the southwest, as though the ship herself had a will to get back to Culebra. I stood watch at the bow, with the great figurehead below me gnashing at the waves.

The fog thickened as we neared the island; it lay like clots of cream oozing from the valleys, flowing to the shore. I felt an urge to brush it from my face, to clear a path that I might see through. Worried that we went too fast, Butterfield had the topsail furled, and no sooner had the men gone aloft than I sighted the island ahead. The gaunt coconut trees were like fingers reaching out, the jungle a blackness behind them. I felt an awful dread to see it all again.

With Horn at the helm, we groped past the point where the shore was steep-to, so close to land that the men on our topsail yard slid above the coconut fronds. The harbour beyond it was a white mass of fog that hid the ships inside, but not the voices of the buccaneers. Their shouts, their shanty, the clacking of their capstan, came disembodied from that fog-filled bay, as though we'd sailed through the skies, from the earth to a world of the dead.

The stern anchor went down, pulling the cable behind

it with a sound like a burning fuse. Then we let the bower go, and snubbed ourselves between them, fixed in place across the harbour entrance, with our broadside looking in.

Abbey went straight to his guns. He greeted them like old friends who had just stopped by to see him. At his direction, we moved the starboard pair across to port, pulling and pushing with rope and spikes. "Come along," Abbey told them. "Come along, my little man-eaters."

His glee chilled me, as did the awful rumble of the carriages, the strain of rope. The sounds would carry through the fog; the buccaneers, I knew, were hearing it, and would know exactly what it meant. Each time we paused to take up the line, I heard the very same sounds coming back through the fog. In this grim and spectral way, our battle was already joined.

The fog began to lift as we brought up the powder and balls for the guns. It thinned along the water, first to the south where the reefs appeared in their petticoats of surf, and then along the island's shore. I saw the rocks at the point, the trees above them, then the dark, hulking shapes of the brig and the schooner. Bows towards us, side by side, they lay not quite together.

I heard the *clack, clack, clack* of a capstan, steady as a clock — unnerving with its rhythm — then saw the men marching round it as the fog lifted over the decks. They warped the brig sideways, on a web of lines stretched to the shore. And the gap between the ships slowly widened; already they were nearly free.

On the *Apostle*, some of the crew were moving one of the long guns towards the bow. Behind it walked half a dozen men, thrusting with their spikes at its wheels, as they might poke at a slow and awkward beast to urge it on its way.

The fog bared the courses on the brig, and then the topsails. It bared the men who worked aloft, repairing the damage I'd caused to rigging and spars. And last of all, before it melted into sunshine, the fog bared the flag atop the *Apostle*'s mainmast, the bloodred flag that meant no quarter.

I stood by at my gun, the lanyard at the ready. As Butterfield paced behind the guns, Abbey sighted each cannon in turn, adjusting the aim with spike and wedge. He laid his cheek against the barrels, squinting with his one good eye straight towards that flag. Then he stepped back, and at his word I tugged the lanyard. The gun leapt towards me as our broadside shuddered through the ship, throwing her sideways like a fighter reeling from a punch. Smoke boiled from the cannons, scattered in the breeze, and wafted back across us with its thick, rough taste of powder. I saw the shot, like four small birds, crashing into the jungle beyond the *Apostle*, one curving off to the right. Abbey had missed, with every ball.

"Now, come on!" he said. It was our aim that was bad, but he kicked the nearest cannon as though to teach it a lesson. "You'll have to do better than that."

Horn leapt to the muzzle of my gun and rammed the

sponge inside. We loaded and fired again. I could *feel* the sound, like a great thump against my chest and head. Abbey grinned. He capered through the whirl of smoke, shouting words I couldn't hear until the ringing left my ears.

"*That's* the *Dragon's* breath," he cried. "That's her smoke and fire." He shook his fist towards the harbour. "Take a whiff of that, you picaroons!"

A hole had appeared, as if by magic, in the topsail of the brig. But the men still worked aloft and, on the deck, the gun kept creeping forward.

Horn was already sponging out the barrel. He glanced towards me with a look as close to fear as I'd ever seen on his face. "That's an eighteen-pounder they're bringing up," he said. "It could sink us like a sieve."

He didn't mean for Abbey to hear. But the gunner did, and he barked up at Horn, "Keep your mouth shut. You know nothing of guns."

"But I've seen what they do." Horn pulled the sponge back and rammed it in, his thick arms bulging. "And God save us if that long one is loaded with chain."

"*You* worry about sponges," said Abbey. "*I'll* worry about guns."

He went off on his business, but Horn's words must have had some effect, for the gunner came back with his spike and hammer. He drove in the wedge to raise the breech, and the muzzle levered down until the gun was nearly level. "We'll aim for the deck," he said. "Let's see how the picaroons work with sixteen pounds of iron flying round them."

He stood behind me, peering over my shoulder as the *Dragon* shifted in the currents, in the wind that was steadily rising. I watched the muzzle waver across the brig, back towards the *Apostle*. The tiny knob at its mouth swung up the shrouds, then down towards the deck. It passed across the group of men who laboured at the cannon.

"Now!" cried Abbey.

I pulled the lanyard. The gun leapt back in a burst of smoke and flames. The powder blew against us, hot and gritty in my eyes. I saw a splash close alongside the *Apostle*, then three others as the guns went off beside me. Two balls fell short and one — poorly made — flew far to the side.

Abbey kicked the gun. "What's wrong with you?" he said, and gave the carriage a clout with his hammer. "You blasted little cannon."

We'd fired twelve rounds and had nothing to show for it but a single hole drilled through a sail. Captain Butterfield stopped his pacing. "Are you shooting at the sharks?" he asked.

Abbey turned to me. "You fired too soon," he said.

"You told me to shoot," I said.

"But you didn't wait." His eye twitched nervously. "Well, never mind. Now we've got the range, Captain. Now we'll blast them to smithereens."

Butterfield scowled. He waited until Abbey had left before he leaned close beside me. "The fellow's as blind as a bat," he said. "He couldn't hit the sponge if it was still in the barrel, but still, I suppose he's doing his best." Then he turned away, and followed Abbey down the row of guns.

Even I could see that Abbey had driven his wedge too far, that the gun was aimed too low. I pulled at the wedge, trying to work it free. But all the weight of the barrel rested on that bit of wood, and I couldn't move it by myself.

Horn put down his sponge. He stood beside me and worked his hands under the barrel. With a grunt he raised it up.

The wedge, suddenly free, seemed to fly from the barrel. I pushed it in, then pulled it halfway out, trying to measure angles in my mind. The muscles stood out on Horn's neck; his face turned red below a grime of powder. But he didn't tell me to hurry; I imagined he didn't have a clue what I was trying to accomplish.

"I've sailed under captains" — he took a breath — "who'd lash you for looking sideways." His lungs emptied and filled. "Captains who never came out of their cabins." His arm muscles doubled in knots. "All have their failings. And Butterfield's is kindness; he's too kind by half."

The wedge was only partly out when the barrel settled on it. "A little more," I said, but Horn shook his head. He was puffing like a bellows. "That will have to do," he told me.

We loaded the gun and hauled it up to the rail. I crouched behind it, watching the little sight drop towards the water. The groundswell passed below us and the sight came slowly up.

Down the length of the gun, across the yards of water, I saw the buccaneers hauling at their cannon, a line of men pulling on a rope. I pulled the lanyard. The flintlock hammered down, its little spark turning all I saw to flames. The tackles sizzled past my feet as the gun recoiled. When the smoke cleared, the buccaneers had scattered.

A cheer went up from our crew. Butterfield said, "Now *that's* good shooting."

"Thank you, sir," said Abbey, with a funny tilting of his head. "I've got us sighted in now, all right."

Horn sneered. He sponged the barrel, and the steam swirled round him. A gun went off beside me, another an instant later, and although the shots were wildly off the mark, they kept the buccaneers at bay. The long gun sat abandoned on the *Apostle*'s deck, but on the brig a dozen men tramped around the capstan, and the gap between the ships grew wider.

Horn rammed the ball down the barrel. "Give them the same again," he said.

I sighted down the gun, the lanyard in my hand. For a moment it dizzied me, the barrel seeming fixed in place as the ships and sky and trees soared across it. The aiming knob settled on the *Apostle*'s deck, on a group of men going boldly to their gun. But I didn't pull the lanyard.

"Shoot," said Horn.

"I can't," I said.

"Don't think of what you're aiming at," said Horn. "They won't give a damn when it's you they see at the end of *their* long gun."

"But it's Dasher," I said.

Directly in my sights, as though he stood atop the knob, was Dashing Tommy Dusker. Like a bright red shield, he'd been brought before the gun, flanked by a pair of buccaneers. It was a twisted little shield he made, hunched down to be as small as he could, but he seemed enormous to me.

"Shoot!" cried Horn.

Chapter 20

A Price to Pay

The *Dragon* rolled in the swell. The muzzle lifted, zooming up the *Apostle's* masts. Then slowly it steadied and started to fall, and Dasher's red coat slashed across the aiming knob. When I pulled the lanyard, there was nothing but water in front of my gun. And the ball fell so pathetically short that a hoot of disdain swelled up from the harbour.

It was a terrible waste of a shot. Horn belittled me with a grim look of anger. "There'll be a price to pay for that," he said.

I glanced back at him, "Dasher saved my life."

"For what?" asked Horn. "Do you think he'd stand there now and want you *not* to shoot?"

"Yes," I cried. He would be a frightened, trembling shield, never believing that I could aim a cannon towards him.

Horn rolled his eyes. "I'm on a ship of fools," he said. "We'll never stop that long gun now."

He was right, but not entirely through my doing. At that moment the brig came free from the *Apostle*. For an instant the two ships leaned together mast to mast. Then they straightened as the brig's long yards untangled from the schooner's shrouds. Within a minute the warping lines were cut, the anchor cable severed. Her courses and topsails were sheeted home and — carried by the tide and wind — the brig came sailing from the harbour.

A mass of men scrambled from her deck. They leapt across the growing gap to the *Apostle*'s rails or took to the boats she had in tow. But they fled from the brig in a tumbling rush. Then only the dead man was left, his arms nailed in place to keep the ship on her course.

Up from the hold came a thin thread of smoke. It twisted through the rigging, swirled around the masts, and rising to the belly of the courses, puffed like little breaths from the edges of the sails.

"They've fired her," said Horn, his back towards me as all of us watched that ship sailing on under a dead man's hand. He whirled round from the rail. "Aim high!" he shouted. "Aim for the masts."

At each of our guns the wedges came out. The barrels lifted like animal snouts, muzzles gaping towards the topsails, which towered higher above us at every moment. Beyond them, deeper in the harbour, the *Apostle* was raising sail.

Abbey came down his line of four little guns; sighting each in turn, giving words of encouragement — not to the men but to the cannons themselves. "Hit her in the sticks," he said. "Shoot straight, you little murderers."

We had time for only one broadside, and we fired the guns as they bore. The sound made a single, ragged clap, the smoke one great, thick cloud. The brig was so close, so big, that it seemed we couldn't possibly miss.

But we did. Two of the balls soared over the ship and one splashed close beside her. The fourth drilled through the topsail but hit nothing but canvas, and the brig came sailing down towards us, wrapped in a thickening smoke. We heard the crackle of the flames, the little bangs of burning timber. We smelled the powder and the wood, the paint and tar. The deck split open down the middle, and the flames — amid a crimson hail of embers — leapt from the holds in a hot and maddened rush.

"Cut the anchors!" shouted Butterfield. "Fore and aft. Abbey, cut them loose." He gazed at the brig, his head tilting higher and higher. Through the hole in her topsail, the smoke blew out in puffs. "Raise the jib," he shouted. "John, you take the helm."

Our small crew scattered throughout the ship. Only Horn was left at the guns, and I saw him bending to his sponge, his broad back taut with muscles. The smoke from the burning brig welled across us, and he vanished in the black and putrid mist.

I ran up to the wheel. I felt the bow swing round as the first anchor was cut away. Then the stern fell free, and the *Dragon* drifted in the currents. She seemed lifeless in my hands.

The brig came swiftly on, so hidden by the smoke that only her mastheads thrust above it. Her courses caught on fire with bursts of yellow flames. Ash and embers rained upon us.

At last I felt the *Dragon* tremble. The jib, filling with wind, gave her life and movement. She slid ahead, and I turned the wheel to meet her.

The brig sailed on, ablaze from end to end. I saw the helmsman at the wheel, his ragged clothes rippling in the tremendous rush of heat. His head, sunk on his chest, lifted for a moment, and the flames caught his clothing, and the smoke welled up to hide him.

The masts, like giants' candles, burned along their lengths. The main yard tilted, broke, and tumbled to the deck. The fire roared with a deafening thunder like a thousand miles of surf rumbling every instant, a thousand rattling carriages on a thousand wooden roads, and all the crowds of London shouting all at once.

The *Dragon* quickened as her foresail filled. She heeled to the hot blasts of wind that came from the brig, driven by the fire itself. I felt the tremble in her rudder and her masts and it seemed to me that she was frightened.

The brig barely missed us. She passed down our port side, so close that I could have leapt and caught her bowsprit. I cringed from heat, from the sound of the fire. My head down, my eyes nearly blinded by smoke, I didn't know who shouted at me; maybe no one did. In all the din and rumble of the fire, the voice that screamed, "Look aloft!" might have come only from my thoughts. But I looked up, and saw the main yard, a flaming sword, slashing for our backstays. I spun the wheel hard and turned us to starboard. The *Dragon* tilted heavily. The brig's long yard scraped across our shrouds and stays.

The yardarm snapped off, hanging by a smouldering brace. Then the fire was behind us, and we sailed from the smoke into sunshine. And directly ahead was the *Apostle*.

She was nearly free from the harbour, bearing down on the wind with her topsail bulging, her boats in tow behind her. On the yard rode her men, brandishing cutlasses that shone in the sun. At her wheel stood Bartholomew Grace. And up in the bow was that long gun, its barrel pointed straight towards us.

In the *Dragon*'s waist, Horn worked alone at the little four-pounder. From sponge to powder, to ball and ram, he went silently through his labours as others raised the topsail.

The *Apostle*'s black hull plunged through the tide rips on the shallow bar. White water leapt at her bow, and high on her yards rode the buccaneers, with tiny glints of gold in their earrings. Above them, the crimson flag stiffened and curled and stiffened again. Below them, the gunners hauled their long gun up to the rail.

Horn threw down his ram and took up the tail of his tackles. He wrapped the rope around his shoulders and, leaning to it, dragged the little cannon forward.

A howl came from the *Apostle*, a cry from the men on her yards. In the steady roar from the burning brig, it was a faint and distant-sounding cry, as though from a pack of dogs running on a moor.

Our topsail filled, the canvas falling, snapping open. It urged the *Dragon* on, and every instinct told me to turn the wheel and put our stern towards that big, black schooner. But Horn, with the smallest gesture, told me to keep her on her course. He lowered his head, and pulled again at the tackles.

When the sails were set, the crew turned from sheets and braces to man the cannons instead. A sailor came aft to take the wheel. "The captain wants you at the guns," he told me.

I ran to the waist. Horn let go of his tackle and stooped to sight the cannon. But Abbey shouldered him aside. "They're mine," he shouted. "You don't know my guns."

Horn stared down at him. His hands, in fists, were as big as sledgehammers. "I was a gunner's mate," he said.

Abbey didn't look up from the sights. "Tell us, Spinner."

"Damn you," said Horn. His voice was low but touched with rage. "For three years I was gunner's mate for that devil, that Bartholomew Grace. Now stand away from that gun, you bloody little fool."

Abbey straightened. It seemed that he meant to give up his place, to surrender his beloved gun. But I saw his hand reach for the lanyard. And I threw myself at him. We fell against the rail as Horn stepped in behind the barrel.

"Hurry," I said.

Horn smiled faintly. "There's no hurrying this, Mr Spencer."

The *Dragon* trembled at the height of a roll; then the deck fell away and the water rushed up to meet us. One hand behind his back, one on the lanyard, Horn sighted down the gun.

Over his shoulder I saw the *Apostle*. Barely a hundred yards away, her bow rose from the swell, pushing foam at either side like rows of gleaming teeth. A puff of smoke burst from the long gun and, on the instant, Horn pulled his lanyard.

The muzzle was right beside me. I was deafened by the noise, blinded by the flames and smoke. I felt the shock of the gun as it crashed back against the tackles. Suddenly there was blood on my arms, and a man was screaming.

"Chain shot," said Horn. "They fired chain at us."

In a moment, our crew had been reduced by two. Our helmsman fell to the deck, and the *Dragon* veered from her course. At the same instant, little Roland Abbey slumped against me with blood spurting from his neck. I staggered back and let him roll past me; I eased him down.

"Did we hit them?" he asked.

Horn was already sponging the barrel. The smoke cleared away, and I saw a great chunk torn from the *Apostle*'s rail, the long gun tipped on its end. The black schooner was turning away.

"Yes," I said. "We hit them for six."

Butterfield knelt beside us. He pressed his hand on Abbey's neck, but the blood flowed up through his fingers.

"Green," said Abbey.

"Hush." I tightened his jacket, for he was starting to shiver. He had taken the shot that was meant to be mine; I had held him there like an offering for the buccaneers' gun. Yet now he smiled at me, his good eye glazing over.

"Green," he said again. "It's the Fiddler's Green. I can see it now." He shuddered and, still smiling, he was gone.

Butterfield, his fingers wet with Abbey's blood, slid the gunner's eyelids closed. "John," he said. "You'll have to take the wheel."

I turned away, but Horn called after me. "Mr Spencer. Keep them off our larboard side. Whatever they do, keep our guns towards them."

Chapter 21

The fire Ship

I had to stand astride the fallen helmsman to take my place at the wheel. His cheek was pressed against the deck, and I was thankful not to see his face. But the way the sun touched his hair — the way his hands lay side by side — filled me with a great pity for the man — and for all of us, but myself most of all.

We had four little cannons, all on one side, and not enough men to work them. The *Apostle* could sail circles round us. With a single broadside she could tear down our masts and leave us a hulk. What would happen then?

I saw myself nailed to the wheel, my corpse steering a dead ship across the ocean as the worms ate it away, month by month. Then I heard, from the waist, the words of our song. It was Horn who started it, but the others joined in, and Butterfield too. In the stirring words to the old "Heart of Oak", I felt my pity vanish. I shook myself and gripped the wheel in my fists.

The *Apostle* was swinging towards us, her boats sledding out on their tow lines. I touched the wheel, and the ships began to circle.

I could see Grace at the helm, the bright dot of his feather. I tried to put myself there, to make his thoughts my own. If I were in his place, I would spare my powder and my shot and herd the *Dragon* towards the reefs, where the sea might do my killing for me. I watched his topsail and saw it shiver, and hoped I'd guessed him right.

I glanced towards the burning brig, then spun the wheel, round and round until the rudder met the stops. The *Dragon* swung her bowsprit across the island, across the surf and the open sea. Her deck at a slant, her sails full, she spun in place like a top.

It caught Grace by surprise. We were like a little dog he was trying to chase towards a corner, suddenly turning to race between his legs. Our guns came to bear for only an instant, but Horn found his mark.

The *Apostle's* foremast snapped in the middle. It leaned and swayed, and the men on the yard clutched the rigging. With a groan and a crack, the topmast finally parted. It hung, for a moment, from the stays and braces. Men tumbled down like a windfallen fruit, and half the mast went behind them, toppling into the sea. The flying jib went with it, and the *Apostle* slewed sideways, in a tangle of rigging and canvas.

Like umbrellas held to the wind, the *Dragon*'s jibs were dragging her down towards the reefs. I straightened the wheel as our men moved from the guns to the sails. Only Horn stayed where he was, sponging and loading, ramming a new ball into the barrel.

The buccaneers cut away their topmast; we freed our sheets and tacked the *Dragon* into the pall of smoke from the burning brig. We sailed right through it, and out to the clear, and the *Apostle* was there ahead of us. She fired a ragged broadside, and the balls whistled past. Again I threw the rudder over, and Horn bent down to his gun.

I couldn't watch for the hit. The brig was carried by the current now, and I had to jibe to pass around her.

But I heard the men cheering in the waist, and when I looked up, I saw the *Apostle* turned head to the wind, all her sails shivering. I guessed that Horn had hit her rudder or cut her steering cables. Certainly he'd struck a mortal blow, for the red flag was gone from her masthead, and up to its place rose a broad white banner mottled with stains of rust. Bartholomew Grace had surrendered.

I joined in the cheering, as loud as any other. But in the waist, Horn and the captain were arguing. They stood chest to chest, until Butterfield turned suddenly away and stalked towards me. Horn came on his heels.

"Strike the topsail!" shouted Butterfield as he came up to the quarterdeck. He stood beside me, taking only a glance at the body on the deck. "We'll go alongside, John," he said.

"Sir, please," said Horn, lumbering behind him. "A white flag means nothing to him, sir."

"It means honour to me," said Butterfield.

"But not to Bartholomew Grace." Horn's face was wracked with anguish. "He'll board us, sir. He'll send fifty men over the rail, and what are we but six? The flag's a ruse, that's all it is. I've seen him do it before."

He stood square in front of Butterfield. His chest, with its muscles knotted in enormous lumps, would be all the captain could see. But Butterfield didn't turn away; he stared straight ahead, as though Horn weren't there. He said, "John, take us alongside."

"Don't" said Horn.

I looked across at the *Apostle*, at the white flag fluttering. Between us lay the brig, drifting down towards the buccaneers under a comet's tail of fire and sparks. I saw then why Grace had surrendered. The tides and the breeze, some strange force of attraction, were drawing the ships together.

"They'll burn," said Butterfield.

"Let them!" cried Horn. Sweat dribbled from his forehead in long streaks through the powder. "Sir, I beg you."

"Enough," said Butterfield. "We're Englishmen, not savages."

Horn clenched his fists even tighter. Shaking from

head to toe, his face scarlet, he stepped towards me. I feared that he would knock me aside and steer us away himself. But he only swept past, and went hurrying down the companionway.

"What if he's right?" I said. "What if this is only a ruse?"

"John, it's a white flag," said Butterfield. But his tongue licked out and touched his lips, and he didn't look at all convinced.

We passed upwind of the brig, through a wave of heat that stirred the air into wild ripples. Then we shortened down to jibs alone, and steered slowly towards the *Apostle*.

Bartholomew Grace stood at the quarterdeck rail, the gold braid of his red coat gleaming in the sunshine and the firelight. I felt a lift in my heart to see Dasher beside him.

Horn bounded up to the deck. He carried a spyglass and the captain's speaking trumpet, which he shoved into Butterfield's hands. "Tell them to take to the boats," he said. "Sir, do that at least. We can pick them up from the boats."

Butterfield stared at the trumpet. Slowly he nodded. "Very well," he said. "Yes, that's fair enough."

"And begging your pardon," said Horn, "but shouldn't we stay out of the reach of their guns?"

"You'll take command yet, won't you?" said Butterfield. But again he nodded. "Pass astern, young John."

Horn stooped to the deck and lifted the dead man

from it. He carried him the way he would carry a sleeping child, and laid him down again beside the rail. Then he stood at my shoulder as I steered towards the *Apostle*'s stern.

We could see Grace very clearly, and Dasher beside him with the old parrot perched on his shoulder. They looked a proper pair of rogues, each as wild as the other. But Dasher lifted a hand and waved with an odd and sad little gesture. His arm stiff, his fingers turning, he looked like a boy waving goodbye to his mother.

Horn put the glass to his eye. "They're chained together," he said.

"Dasher and Grace?"

"Aye." He adjusted the spyglass. "Wrist to wrists. He looks frightened, your friend."

He offered me the glass, but I shook my head; I didn't want to see any more than I already could.

Captain Butterfield wiped his mouth with the back of his hand, then held the trumpet to his lips. "Do you strike your colours?" he shouted.

Bartholomew Grace grabbed a backstay and stepped up on the rail. Behind him, Dasher's hand lifted on the chain. "We do!" said Grace, his voice barely reaching us. "Haul alongside, Captain."

"Take to your boats," said Butterfield. "We'll pick you up from your boats."

Horn grunted. "He's angry, sir. The look he gave you could melt my glass."

"Do you hear me?" shouted Butterfield.

Grace turned away to talk to his crew. With every gesture he made, Dasher's hand — like a puppet's — moved on the chain. We drew level with *Apostle*'s stern, and I luffed up, the sails slattering.

Someone passed a trumpet up to Grace. "Captain," he said. "You'll have to come alongside."

"The devil take you, sir," said Butterfield. He lowered the trumpet. "John, steer clear."

I turned the wheel. We started forward, gathering way.

"Heave to!" shouted Grace. "You'll not sail away on me." His voice rose to a scream. "Heave to, I tell you."

We carried on, slipping through the water as the strengthening tide bore us all to the east. Another burst of embers flurried from the brig as the mizzen collapsed in a fiery web of rigging. Horn swivelled with his spyglass as we left the *Apostle* astern.

"Watch it," he said. And then, "John! Come about."

I turned us into the wind. Horn snapped his glass shut and sprinted down the deck. He ran to the cannons, calling for Butterfield to help him. I looked aft to see the *Apostle* turning, her useless sails suddenly sheeted and braced, her rudder, which I'd thought broken, swinging her round in a fury. She cast away her boats, and a dreadful howl rose from the crew as the buccaneers came after us.

I saw the guns poking out, half-naked men crouching behind them. I held the wheel over, battling tops, our masts tilting steeply. If we'd waited a moment later, her whole broadside would have faced us. But still she got two guns to bear, and the balls — with frightening shrieks — hammered into the longboat atop our cabin. Horn fired with his last shot, straight towards her stern. Even Abbey couldn't have missed, and I watched her transom and her rudder shatter into pieces.

Our jibs came across and we bore away, through a narrowing gap between the *Apostle* and the brig. We'd sailed just a hundred yards when the fire ship exploded.

Chapter 22

Bound for England

A wall of heated air knocked us onto our side. Planks and spars soared aloft in a tumbling cloud, and the grenades ignited like a rumble of thunder. A ball of fire spread from the brig as one explosion followed another, and the blazing wreck vanished from the world. It left the *Apostle* mastless and sinking, a smoking hulk already down to her deck in the sea.

The sharks came, and the water seemed to bubble round her. It rose over the rail and swept among the guns; it gushed in spouts from her hatches. Then the *Apostle* tilted up at the stern and slid forward with an awful quickness, as though the sea were pulling her in. The boats went down behind her, and by the time we turned the ship, there was nothing left but scraps of floating wood.

Huge eddies came up from below, dark swirls that opened like funnels. They tossed the *Dragon* to port and to starboard, and the sharks raced round and round. There wasn't a man to be seen.

"The suction," said Horn. "It will hold them all down. Davy Jones won't give up one of that lot."

But he did. A head bobbed from the water, then a mass of red. And Dasher floated beside us with his wineskins inflated. His crimson coat was like a whirl of blood, into which he sank, then rose again. Bartholomew Grace was beside him, his face hidden by the drooping brims of his hat. They were still chained wrist to wrist.

A familiar voice, so cheery that I almost wept, shouted from below, "Lively, lads. Haul away, boys. It's Dashing Tommy Dusker you've got, and he'll make rich men of you all."

Hands reached over and dragged him up over the rail. His big wineskins were bunched around his shoulders. They squeaked as he tugged them down with his one free hand. He posed for a moment, as sodden as a rat, then knelt and kissed the deck.

It was meant to be a show of great drama, but his chained arm was pulled behind him, and poor Dasher only toppled forward until his nose was squashed against the planks. "Oh, the *Dragon*," he said. "The blessed *Dragon*, come all this way to find me."

No one paid him any mind. We dragged Bartholomew Grace aboard, and let the buccaneer tumble over the rail. He landed with a thud, his fine clothes in disarray, his feathered hat crushed below him. He braced himself with a horrid hand, a crab's claw scorched long ago to nothing more than skin and bones.

"That one you can throw back," snarled Butterfield. "Davy Jones won't rest until he has him."

The anger in my uncle Stanley's voice surprised me. Even more did the lack of anger in the voice of Horn, who — alone among us — begged to keep the buccaneer aboard. "It's my only chance," he said. "He has to stand trial."

Grace rolled onto his side, and for the first time I saw his face close at hand. It was blotched with patches of livid white and patches of pink, like the skin of a plucked chicken. Melted by that long-ago fire, healed into a nightmarish blob, the villain's face had only a hole where his nose should have been, and shrivelled black worms for lips.

"There's still a fortune on that island," said Dasher. "Riches tucked away. What say you, lads? Shall we go ashore and fetch it?"

He might have been talking to himself. From the captain on down we stood and stared at Bartholomew Grace, and the hideous mask that turned to meet us. One of his eyes was higher than the other, but both seemed to bulge from his cheeks. He found Horn and looked up.

"You," he said. "I should have killed you outright. I should have torn your heart out and fed it to the fish." He sat up, snarling like a dog. "You've lost the treasure and sunk the ship. What's next, Horn? What misfortune will you bring?"

"The hangman for you," said Horn. He bent down and stretched the chain between his hands.

"And for yourself? A deserter." Grace winced as Horn wrenched the chain to free him from Dusker. "If you're lucky, they'll only flog you round the fleet. A thousand lashes, until your yellow backbone's standing out for all to see."

Again Horn wrenched the chain violently. The links stretched and bent. With a grunt, he snapped the chain in two.

"There's another way," said Grace. "Come a-roving. All of you." His terrible eyes shifted from Horn to Butterfield to Mudge, then to me. "Lad," he said, "don't you wish for that? You'd be as free as the wind, the sea for your home. No man you'd call a master, no country to call you slave. You'd live a life full of riches, a journeyman of the sea with the cutlass and the cannon for your tools. Come buccaneering, boy; don't you dream of that?"

"I dream of seeing you hanged," said I, though in truth his little speech had stirred my soul. And by the shuffling feet of the men around me, I knew he'd touched others with the same vision.

"It's a fine life," he said, as though I hadn't spoken. He

drew himself up until he sat with his back to the rail. He talked directly to Mudge. "Everyone's equal on a ship of fortune. There's no 'aye, sir, no, sir' when it comes to buccaneering." He turned to Butterfield. "There's no slaving away for a company owner. Each is his own man." To me he said, "You go where the wind takes you. Where a fortune waits for the finding." And last he turned to Dasher. "If you've got the heart for it. If you're man enough to be a lord of the ocean."

There was danger in his words, in the way he somehow addressed them straight to the heart of every soul. If we'd given Grace his head, he might have turned us all to piracy, for other eyes began to glimmer at his words. But Butterfield cut him short.

"You can tell all that to the jury," he said. "Maybe *they* will care, but I don't give a fig." He stepped back and motioned to a pair of men, George Betts and Harry Freeman. "Take the cur down below. Chain him in the Cave."

Bartholomew Grace put up no fight. But he shouted after Horn as the sailors led him away.

"You'll hang with me," he said. "Side by side; I'll see to that."

His shouts grew louder as Betts and Freeman hurried him off. "You think you can buy your freedom with me? Why, we'll swing in chains, Horn. We'll swing together, you and I."

His voice became a scream. "They don't forgive deserters, Horn."

He looked back for an instant as the men shoved him down the hatch. His clawed hand came up and pointed at us. "Damn this ship and every man. This I swear: you'll never see your homes again. By the laws of Oleron, I damn you all to Davy Jones."

He seemed to sink within the ship. The men followed him down, and there was only the echo of his voice, and a chill that descended on us all.

Dasher clapped his hands. "Right, then. Who's the captain here?"

Butterfield looked surprised. I imagined that his ears — like mine — still rang with the haunting curses of Bartholomew Grace.

"Speak up," said Dasher. "Who's the Captain Hackum, eh? Who's the lucky cove?"

Uncle Stanley frowned. "I'm Captain Butterfield," he said.

"Bless your heart," crowed Dasher. He was grinning widely. "You'll thank your stars for the day you pulled me from the sea."

Butterfield's frown deepened into furrows. "And who the devil are you?"

Dasher looked at me, his grin fading. "Didn't you tell them, John?"

"I did," said I. "Captain, this is Dasher."

Butterfield smiled. He shook Dasher's hand. "Sir, I'm in your debt," he said.

"Not 'sir'," cried Dasher. "Not yet. Now, take me back to

the island and I'll line your pockets with so much silver you'll need a cable to hold your trousers up."

"The island?" asked Butterfield.

"Well, won't it turn?"

"Aye, and then turn again. We'd be trapped in there for a day or more."

"A boat," said Dasher. "I'll nip in with a boat, fetch the silver, and nip out again."

"In that?" Butterfield pointed to the shattered longboat. It was the only one we had. "Make all sail," he shouted, turning his back on Dasher. "We're bound for England."

"Captain!" Dasher cried. "John, tell him about my treasure."

I followed on Butterfield's heels down the companionway. "Sir," I said. "It's true. He's got a barrel full of gold and silver."

Butterfield stepped into his cabin. He bent over his chart table and picked up his pencil and parallel rules.

"Couldn't we wait and get it?" I asked. "We've time enough for that."

"I'm sorry, John." He laid a course between the reefs, then walked his rule towards the compass rose.

"But, sir," I said. "It means everything to Dasher."

"Which is precisely why we'll leave it where it lies." He marked his course in pencil, then clapped the rule together. "You know what the Good Book says about money."

"It's the root of all evil," I said.

He shook his head. "No, John. The *love* of money is the root of all evil. And a truer word was never written." He looked up at me, his kindly face worn by worry. "Think of the misery that's tied to that treasure. The horror in collecting it; the deaths from searching for it. I think it best we leave it where it is, don't you?"

He looked at me across the table, and smiled sadly. "You disagree. Well, we *shall* leave it where it is. No matter what you think."

I went up on deck and found Dasher at the rail. He was staring at Culebra as it passed beside us. I told him we wouldn't be stopping.

"I thought not," he said. "I had a feeling in my bones."

The chain dangled from his wrist, tapping on his boots as the *Dragon* rolled. Our guns were drawn up to the rails, lashed in place with heavy lines. Horn and another man were throwing the remains of the longboat over the side.

"I'll never get rich, I won't," said Dasher. "Blast my luck."

"What will you do now?" I asked.

"Oh," he sighed. "I suppose I'll pick a few pockets, try to set up a stake. Maybe I'll buy one of those dancing bears and go waltzing across England. Maybe I'll take to the stage; I'd make a fine actor, don't you think?"

"You would," I said.

"And at least I've had my fling. I've had my grand adventure."

"There's still the glory," I said.

"Well, your Captain Hackum will get that now. His little ship and his little guns rid the sea of pirates... There's glory for you. Yes, I've lost that too."

"And your parrot," I said. "I'm sorry."

"That blithering little idiot? I'm glad to see the last of him."

Dasher turned his back on Culebra. He went off to find a chisel and a hammer, and we sailed on, south around the island, north past Luis Peña Cay. The mosquitoes there were so thick that I saw them from half a mile away, a grey smudge above the beaches. We left all the land astern, then hove to in the open ocean, to bury our dead in a sad little ceremony.

Captain Butterfield read from the Bible. The dead helmsman and Roland Abbey lay on the deck, the sun shining on their shrouds of white canvas. I squeezed the old gunner's shoulder and hoped he was already in Fiddler's Green, among his taverns and his trees. Then I walked away so that I wouldn't have to watch him sink into such a depth of water, and I covered my ears to keep from hearing the splashes. For the first time, I cried for poor Mr Abbey.

We steered for home with the trades blowing over the quarter. They blew so fair and so steady that our braces and sheets hardened in their blocks, for we never trimmed a sail. The *Dragon* seemed to run on rails, and a great current — a river in the ocean — swept us along our way.

It was a romp across a rolling sea. Our watches changed, and changed again, and our life was leisurely and content. I took on the task of caring for Bartholomew Grace, feeding him — like an animal — twice a day in the darkness of the Cave. I found him sulky at times, angry at times, but he would always thank me for what I'd brought him, and ask about our progress. I was careful not to get too close, and only prodded my offerings towards him.

In six days we were north of Bermuda, turning steadily east as the westerlies filled to carry us home. Dasher joined in the work as though he'd always been a part of the crew. He scrubbed the decks and stood his turns at the wheel. But he never went aloft, and he never took the air from his wineskins. They made him fat and awkward, afraid to climb the rigging.

On the seventh, Butterfield aimed his bent sextant at the sun as it rose above the bowsprit. He stood with one leg stiff, the other bending to the *Dragon*'s roll. I waited with my book, ready to write down the angles as he called them out.

"Oh, my," he said. "Goodness."

"What's the matter?" I asked.

He lowered the sextant. He put his hand over his brow, and swayed on his feet.

"John, I feel poorly," he said.

The next thing I knew, he was slumped on the deck, with the sextant lying beside him.

Chapter 23

A Gentleman of Fortune

"Uncle Stanley," I said. It scared me to see him stricken so suddenly, and I became a child again, shouting for help, nearly crying as I pushed at his shoulders.

He trembled at my touch, sloshing in his clothes like a bag of water, as though all his bones were disconnected. His skin was hot and clammy.

"Help!" I cried again, and Horn came running. Dasher was closer, but he stopped short a yard away.

"Lord, he's dead. He's hopped the twig," he said.

Horn pushed him aside. He knelt beside me and ran his hands over the captain's chest, up his neck to his cheeks, to his forehead. He pried the lids from

Butterfield's eyes, and I saw the whites underneath — only the whites — and gasped at the shock of it.

"Steady, John," said Horn. "He's got the fever. That's all it is."

"The fever!" cried Dasher. He covered his mouth with his hand, pinching his nostrils shut. "How did he get it out here?"

"He didn't," said Horn. "It's been inside him since Luis Peña Cay."

"We all might get it," said Dasher through his fingers.

Horn shook his head. "Not you, and not young John. But the rest of us, aye. The ones who went ashore at Luis Peña Cay."

"Did you go ashore?" I asked.

"I did," said he. And his words struck me dumb. "You're the master now, Mr Spencer."

By the evening, two other men had been sent down to their hammocks with the shakes and the chills. Apart from Dasher, only Horn and I and the oxlike Mudge were left to work the ship. And the wind was rising as the sun went down.

"Should we reef?" I asked.

"You're the master," said Horn again.

"But should we?" I said. It was my childhood game, but played in earnest now. Horn annoyed me with his silence.

"Tell me," I said.

He frowned at the sails. "Who can say, Mr Spencer? If

you reef, you slow the ship; if you don't, you gamble with the wind. It's a decision for the master, not a sailor."

"Then we'll furl the main," I said, "and carry on."

"Aye, aye," said Horn. He smiled. "That's just what I would do."

Dasher steered as we wrestled with the canvas. With Horn on one side of the boom, Mudge and I on the other, we dropped the main in its lazy jacks. And the *Dragon*, stripped of her largest sail, ran before the wind from twilight into darkness.

I sent Mudge below and gave the watch to Horn. "I'll look in on the captain," I said.

The lamp was burning low above my uncle's chart table. It swung and squeaked and tossed its shadows through the cabin. But after the darkness on deck, the room seemed full of light to me, and I saw the captain very clearly, wedged behind the weatherboard that had been put in place to keep him in his bunk. White fingers clutched at the edge. A white face stared over the top.

"Who are you?" he asked. His voice was small and frightened.

"It's me," I said. "It's John."

"John?" he asked. "Come closer, boy. Come closer."

I squatted by the bunk. His hand crawled up from the board and seemed to feel at the air. I saw that every move was agony for him, and he closed his eyes as he groped to find my shoulder. I took his hand; it was hot as embers.

"I'm cold," he said. "So cold."

I pulled the blankets round him as I held his hand in mine. His hair was matted with sweat, tightened into little curls. His face was so drawn that I couldn't bear to look at it.

"Did you reef?" he asked.

"Yes," I said. "Don't worry." I squeezed his hand and added, "She can handle her sails."

I'd hoped to brighten him with our old game, but he was too far gone for that. "Of course she can," he said. "She's a good ship. Just keep her running straight."

"I will," I said.

"And listen... listen, boy," he said, as though my name escaped him. "See what Mr Abbey's doing out there."

"Out where?" I asked.

"At the windows, boy. He's tapping at the windows."

"He's not," said I. "He's—"

"Quickly!"

I did as he asked; I saw no harm in it. I walked aft to the big stern windows, where the shadows of the lamp swayed across the curtains. I heard water rushing past the rudder and under the counter, the creaking of the steering ropes, a faint moan of wind through the rigging and the woodwork. The curtains shifted as the *Dragon* moved, and their weighted hems ticked and tapped against the windowpanes.

"Oh, bring him in," said Butterfield.

I reached out to draw the curtains apart. And despite myself, I felt a twinge of fear. The fancy struck me that I *would* see Abbey there, his shroud falling off him, his bloated face grinning through the glass.

"Hurry," said my uncle.

I snatched the curtains open. There was nothing there but the sea, a great darkness broken by ghostly swirls in the *Dragon's* wake. A light splatter of spray fell across the glass. I turned the latch and pushed the windows open.

The wind came in, gusting at the curtains. It whirled through the cabin and breathed against the lamp until the flame grew large, then small. I smelled the salt water and a trace of the land far behind us. Then Butterfield said, "There, that's better. Where have you been, Mr Abbey?"

I closed the windows and turned around. Butterfield had risen to his elbow and was staring off into the shadows by the bunk. "You're so wet, so white, Mr Abbey."

It sent shivers through me to hear the captain talking to a dead man. I tried to soothe him again, but he only waved me off. "Leave us, boy," he said.

I went straight to my cabin, but sleep escaped me. The motions of the *Dragon* grew steadily worse until my bunk was like a seesaw. Above the sounds of the *Dragon* I heard the clanking of the buccaneer's chains from deep in the Cave. I heard Butterfield talking away, with long pauses between his sentences, and now a laugh and now an "Aye! That's right, Mr Abbey." Finally I dressed again and went wearily aloft.

Horn and Dasher both stood at the wheel. They leaned back, staring up, driving the ship — as she reared and plunged — like a pair of charioteers. Dasher's long coat flapped and tangled at the spokes.

The deck was a hill that I had to climb to reach them, then a slope that I staggered down. I grabbed the binnacle and stared at the compass. We were running south by east.

"I don't care for this," said Dasher. "I don't care much for this at all."

Horn smiled. "Oh, she'll do all right. It's only a squall."

"And it's only a pond we have to cross," said Dasher. "Lord love me, I'd rather be locked up in the madhouse right now. It's where I ought to be, I think."

"And miss the sea?" asked Horn. "Miss the wind and the feel of a ship? Wouldn't you miss all that, my friend?"

"That's all I'd miss — the misses," said Dasher. "But I'd still have idiots for company."

The *Dragon* shuddered then, as the bow dug into the sea. I looked up at the straining topsail. "I'd like to reef," I said.

"But how?" asked Horn. "Mudge down below, just you and I and a landsman on the deck."

"Who's the landsman, then?" said Dasher. But he laughed. He made no bones about his calling, and never shed his landsman's clothes — the boots and the flapping coat — nor the wineskins strapped tightly across his chest.

"There's Grace," I said. "We could bring him from below."

"No," cried Horn, and for a moment his blue eyes burned. "Don't think of that, Mr Spencer. He's like a witch, I tell you. If he's ever freed from those chains, if his feet ever touch this deck, he'll find a way to ruin us."

"If he's not already drowned," said Dasher.

The foredeck ran with water. Black seas tumbled aboard, breaking against the capstan, gurgling at the hawse. I hadn't gone once that day to the door of the Cave.

"Just keep her before the wind," said Horn. "The squall will pass by daybreak."

I nodded. "Very well." If Horn wasn't worried, there was no need for worry. I went below and filled a bucket with bread and cheese and scraps of meat. I added a flask of water, took a lantern from its peg, and carried it all to the doorway at the end of the Cave.

I hammered on the wood. "Captain Grace!" I shouted. "Get back from the door."

His chains clanked. I set down my bucket and turned the latch. The door creaked open.

It was that moment I feared the most. I couldn't open the door without thinking that Grace would come crashing through it, loosed from his chains. I steeled myself to slam it shut again, then held my lantern out, and thrust it through the door.

The Cave stank of sweat and waste. It echoed with the sounds of the sea and the creak of the timbers and the thunder from the figurehead. It was the vilest prison I might imagine, always moving, pitching, with the passage of the ship. Bartholomew Grace sat huddled at the edge of my lamplight his back against the planking, his feet against the wall. His face seemed ghastly white; a week had passed without his seeing the sun.

He turned that face towards me. His lopsided eyes and burnt-away lips, the hole for his nose — I was always shocked to see them. But now I found a pity for him, within my hatred and my fear.

"I've brought you food," I said.

His eyes shifted only briefly towards my bucket. "We've turned to the south," he said.

It amazed me that he knew that.

"And you carry too much sail, so you must be short of hands."

He seemed to wait for an answer, but I wouldn't tell him he was right. I pushed the bucket towards him.

Grace reached out to take it, his clawlike hand catching on the rim. I moved back from the door. "Is it the fever?" he asked. "Have you got it yourself?"

I shook my head. His horrible gaze studied me before dropping to the bucket. He took out the water and drained half the flask. Then he started on the food and the bread bubbled in clots round his teeth.

"Has the captain got it?" he asked.

"Give me the bucket," I said.

He nudged it a bare inch towards me. I would have to crawl into the passage to reach it.

"I hear him talking to himself," said Grace. "He's gone

off his head, hasn't he?" He saw that I would give no answer. "Who's to navigate? Who's to find our way?" He took the cheese and gnawed at the edge. "Not you; I'll tell you that."

The *Dragon* pitched violently. The empty bucket tipped on its bottom as a loud crack of timbers sounded from the bow. Grace turned his head, and I reached out and snatched the bucket. Something like anger blazed in the buccaneer's eyes.

"You'll stagger across the ocean, boy," he said. "You'll be chased by one wind, followed by another, and you'll dare do nothing but run before them. Then you'll meet a gale, or a helmsman will let her broach, and you'll lose a mast or drive her under."

"We'll take our chance," I said.

"Rid me of these shackles, boy. Let me loose and I'll make a rich man of you. A gentleman of fortune."

"I don't wish to be a picaroon," I said.

The word incensed him. "Damn your blood!" he shouted. "You little cur. You'll bring the ship to ruin, *then* you'll come and fetch me. You'll beg me for my help."

I drew back from the door. "Good day to you, Captain Grace," I said.

He wrenched at his chains. He pulled so violently, with such a rage, that I was sure he'd tear the ringbolts from the deck. I retreated with my bucket and my lantern.

"Run!" he said, and clanked his chains. He laughed.

I closed the door on Bartholomew Grace. But his voice came clearly through the wood.

"I shan't be chained for ever, boy. And my vengeance shall be terrible."

Chapter 24

A Ghostly Visit

In the hours before dawn, the ghost of our gunner went over the side. Poor Abbey's spirit, if it had ever come in by the windows, was gone by daylight, when we set the *Dragon* again on her proper course.

The squall had passed, without ever rising to the gale I'd feared. And we sailed on towards England, across a sea that was like a field of boulders, so round and jumbled were the waves.

Horn went below and tossed Mudge from his hammock. He pushed him up the ladder and kicked him down the deck. The fat sailor hopped like a toad, scratching himself awake, then wrapped his clumsy hands around the spokes of the *Dragon's* wheel.

We left her in his care, and went below to sleep. But I stopped by the captain's cabin, where I found Butterfield wide awake, lying on his back on his bunk.

"John," he said happily. "Come in."

"Is there anyone with you?" I asked.

He frowned. "What a deuced silly question. Who could be with me, John?"

It cheered me greatly to see him back in his senses. He remembered nothing of the night, imagining that he had slept right through it, and I didn't tell him that Abbey's ghost had made a visit.

"I'm tired," he said. "And sore all over. But I'd like a bit of breakfast, I think."

I looked up at the skylight. "Mudge is steering," I said.

"Blast." He took a long breath and sighed it out. "Well, perhaps I'll wait."

I went to my cabin and fell asleep in an instant, rocked by the *Dragon* as she tumbled from wave to wave. I was still sleeping at noon, when Butterfield took a sextant sight and placed us twenty leagues south of our course. I slept until midafternoon, when I finally turned myself out and found Horn at the wheel again, humming his song. He nodded towards the skylight, and I looked down to see Butterfield feasting on cheese and jam-clotted bread. It didn't surprise me that Dasher was there, tucking in like a starving man. I felt a twinge of jealousy not to be with them.

"The captain looks better," I said.

"For now," said Horn.

His answer puzzled me.

"That's the way the fever works. A day from now, a week from now, he might be flat on his back again."

I saw the truth in this as the days went by, as the miles passed under our keel. The sailors who had gone ashore on Luis Peña Cay recovered from their fevers, only to be stricken again. Then Mudge took to his hammock, claiming he had the chills.

Dasher suspected that he didn't. "It's a sham," he said. "He's a cunning cove, isn't he?" He shook his head and set his hair flying around his shoulders. "Sharp's the word with him. Oh, Lord, I should have thought of it myself."

But Dasher never shirked his duties. He steered the ship and trimmed the sails, always in his flowing coat, always in his wineskins. We couldn't cross the ocean fast enough for him, and he loved to learn our progress from noon to noon, then change it to a distance that he knew.

"A hundred and fifty miles," he'd say, grinning. "Why, we've just gone from Ramsgate to Portsmouth. Maybe more." And then, "Fancy that. I've never been to Portsmouth."

He despaired in the calms and trembled in the squalls. He hated to see the *Dragon* turn from her course, but we always ran before the wind, when it rose, because Horn had doubts about the rigging.

"You see how the foremast shakes?" he asked me during one of the squalls. And indeed it did. When the wind was high, it trembled more than Dasher. It shook with a little rattle in its partners, where it came up through the deck, with a low hum that grew louder with each passing squall.

"Will it break?" I asked.

"Not if we run," said Horn. "Not if we keep the wind astern."

So we let the wind chase us, as Grace had said. The crosses on the captain's chart made a jagged line, and once a loop when the wind came suddenly from the east. But they inched towards England. And there were only three hundred miles to go — "Dover to Devon," said Dasher, gloating — when Butterfield took a turn for the worse.

I had just given Grace his evening meal; I was putting the latch into place when I heard the captain behind me.

"Who's that you've got in there?" he asked.

"Don't you remember, Uncle?" said I. "It's Bartholomew Grace."

He repeated the name as though he'd never heard it before. "And why is he berthed in the Cave?"

I took his arm. "You said to put him there. He came from the *Apostle*, remember?"

"Yes, of course," he said, though clearly he'd forgotten. "How silly of me." He touched his forehead. "I'm afraid I don't feel quite right today."

I led him back to his cabin and got him settled in his bunk. In the morning he greeted me warmly, much to my relief.

"John," he said when I came to his door. "Come in, come in, young man. I have some news to tell you."

I sat at the foot of his bunk. He looked tired but otherwise healthy.

"Listen, John," he said. "Your father came by to see me last night."

My heart sank, and it must have shown on my face. Butterfield laughed. "No, no," he said." It's not bad news. He could only stay a moment, just a moment, but he wanted to say how proud you have made him. He bids you Godspeed, and is anxious to see you again."

The thought struck me — I couldn't help it — that my father had died, that his ghost, like Abbey's, had come aboard the *Dragon*. "Did you let him in by the windows?" I asked.

"Of course not," said Butterfield. "What rubbish you speak. He came through the skylight, John."

I left his cabin feeling troubled and sad. But Dasher greeted me on deck with a hearty laugh.

"Oh, ho!" he said. "Why the long face? You'll trip on your chin if you don't lift your head."

"It's the captain," I said.

"What's wrong with him?"

"Go and look for yourself."

So Dasher went below, and even he came back disheartened. "Your Captain Hackum's lost his wits," he said. He mocked Butterfield's voice: "'Dashing Tommy what?' Strike me dead, you'd think he never heard of me."

For the first time in our homeward voyage, noon came and went without Butterfield's taking a sextant sight. Dasher ached to know how far we'd gone, and asked me, "Can't you do it yourself?"

"No," I said. "I never learned."

"Get Horn to do it, then."

That was his answer to everything, and somehow it annoyed. But I called Horn aft and told him our problem. "Will you take the sight?" I asked.

"You're the master, Mr Spencer," said Horn. "I'll do anything you tell me, but I can't do that."

"Why not?" I snapped.

"I'm lost when it comes to numbers." He lowered his head. "I'm just a seaman, Mr Spencer. Just a lowly seaman and never more than that."

"You said—"

"Yarns, Mr Spencer. I was too thick to make an officer."

Suddenly he seemed smaller, less than perfect, just a model of the man I'd known.

"But you do know how to navigate," I said. "You were steering your boat for Africa."

"Was I on course?" he asked.

I shrugged. "I don't know."

"Nor do I." He shrank even more. "I can't read, Mr Spencer. I can't even write my name."

I remembered the bird he'd drawn in the log, the albatross that now seemed real enough to be hanging round my neck.

"Why, I could no more find our way to England," said Horn, "than I could dance a quadrille at Windsor Castle."

Dasher laughed. It was his high, sickly laugh, which I'd heard only in moments of peril. "Well, that's a fine kettle of fish," he said. "There's a pretty piece of business for you."

"Be quiet," I snapped. It seemed everything we'd done, every action we'd taken, was like a domino stood upon a table. There was Horn coming aboard, and Abbey with his guns, the slave trader in Jamaica, and the *Apostle* in the storm. And they were falling now, one knocking against the other, our whole voyage tumbling into ruin.

"Who's to navigate?" asked Dasher, echoing the words of Bartholomew Grace: *Who's to navigate? Who's to find our way? Not you; I'll tell you that.*

"Well?" he asked. "What about Grace?"

His question hung in the air. What about Grace?

"Put the sextant in his mitts and point him at the sun, I say." Dasher's wineskins squeaked as he shrugged. "What choice do we have?"

Horn shook his head slowly. His face was a picture of agony, as though he blamed all our misfortune on the single fact that he'd never learned his numbers. He quoted a Bible verse, perhaps the only one he knew. "'The wolf... shall dwell with the lamb.'"

I finished it for him. "'And a little child shall lead them.'" I was no longer a child, though I wasn't half the age of either Horn or Dasher. But I would have to do it, I thought. I would have to learn.

I went below and brought up the sextant and chronometer, the tables and books. I brought the broad chart of the North Atlantic, and I spread it all out on the deck, the books to weight the chart in place. Then I took the sextant from the box and held it like a talisman. I willed it to tell us where we were.

Butterfield had made it look so easy. In seconds, he could find the sun in the sextant's little telescope, moving its image in the mirror until it balanced on the skyline. But I stood there for an hour as everything I saw zoomed and tilted in ways I wouldn't have thought possible. I no sooner brought the sun down to the horizon than it slipped away and I had to start all over.

Every move of the ship seemed doubled in the sextant, then reversed by the mirror, and I nearly came to tears before I suddenly got it right and read the angle from the scale. Then I did it again, and a third time, just as Butterfield would have, and took the middle of the three.

All my life, my father had trained me for his business. I had worked with numbers and loathed them. I had fought against him, determined to get to sea and escape the prison of his office. Now I blessed him for his teachings as I puzzled my way through the almanac and logarithms. Finally I said, "Handy-dandy, here's where we be," and touched the chart.

Dasher stared at my finger, then squinted at the sea. "I've been to France," he said. "It didn't look like this."

I'd put us in the middle of Europe. "I can't do it," I said.

"We'll just carry on until we bump into land," said Dasher. "How far wrong can we go if we aim for Ushant?"

"But we don't know where we are," I said. "That's the problem. How can you aim at something if you don't know where you're aiming from?"

"You can't miss all of Europe," said Dasher. "You have to hit the land."

"Yes," I said. "Like Admiral Shovell."

"Who?"

"Sir Clowdisley." He had been taking a squadron home to England a hundred years before. A sailor had warned him that he'd lost his way and all the ships were in peril. Admiral Shovell hanged the sailor for his trouble, then kept his course, straight onto the Scilly Isles. "Four ships were lost," I said. "And all their men but two."

Dasher tugged at his wineskins. He patted them to test their fullness. "Then you'd better learn," he said.

I took a dozen sights and went through the reductions step by step. The *Dragon* sailed along, seven miles in every hour, seven hundred feet per minute. I heard the water rushing past her hull, swirling at the counter, and I knew I had to get it right or all of us might perish.

Chapter 25

Storm Canvas

"Get back from the door," I shouted that evening as I stood at the entrance to the Cave with my bucket and my lantern. I waited for the clank of chain, but there was no sound from within.

"Captain Grace!" I kicked the door. "Answer me," I said.

There was only silence. The *Dragon* lay slightly on her starboard side, holding a course to the east in a northerly breeze. My lamp cast shadows on the tilted planks and seemed to lean precariously when I set it flat on the deck.

I put my ear to the door and listened. I heard breaths, steady and slow, as though Grace had his own ear to the other side. My heart quickened at the thought of him waiting there, just an inch away. Then the deck tilted sharply and the breathing changed its pattern. I thought it was only the sea that I heard, the faint surge of water carried through the wood.

"Captain Grace," I called again. I drew the latch as quietly as I could and threw the door open. Grace sat just where I'd left him, staring at me from the edge of the lamplight. His nose was a gaping hole in the shadows, but his eyes shone like fires.

"Why didn't you speak?" I said.

"I had nothing to say," he told me.

He sat on top of his chains, the ringbolts in the deck hidden by his coat. I had a sudden thought that he wasn't chained at all.

"I brought you a treat," I said, reaching in the bucket. "An orange."

He smiled grotesquely, with nothing but malice. "You're too good to me," he said.

I held it up. "Move back. I want to see your chains."

He barely shifted his hips. "Farther," I said.

He snarled. It was a terrible sound, brimming with evil. But he shuffled back, and I smelled the dampness in his coat, the salty air rotting the cloth from his back. He moved away until I saw the chains and the bolts, everything in place, and he glared at me with utter loathing.

I rolled the orange towards him, and he snatched it up like a beast. He held it in his burned hand and tore the peel away with his teeth.

"Who's navigating?" he asked.

"I am."

"Where are we?"

"I can't tell you that," I said.

He snorted. "You don't know. And you brought me an orange hoping that I'd tell you how to work a sight." He spat out a chunk of peel. "You little whelp; you're holding the ship as far to the north as you can. You're afraid you'll miss the Channel."

He'd guessed close enough to the truth. We were keeping to the north to be sure of sighting England instead of France. And I *was* hoping he'd help me.

"You'll stumble on the land, in the dead of night as like as not. You'll see a point all tossed by surf and you won't know if it's Ireland or England or France."

"We'll know," I said.

"You won't." He tore off another chunk of orange. "The weather's changing, boy. By the time another day has passed, you won't see the sun for clouds. You'll never see it again. The north winds will push you into the Bay of Biscay, onto a lee shore as wild as any. Claw your way off that?" He crushed the orange in his fist. It crumpled inward, spurting juice. "You'll wreck her, boy. You'll kill us all."

I stared at the orange in his hand. He squeezed it harder, until it was just a crumpled bit of skin that he cast down on the deck. It rolled over as the *Dragon* heeled. The wind was already rising.

"You'd be the first to drown," I said.

Grace laughed. "First or last, what difference does it make? We'll all drown if you don't get a sight by morning."

We glared at each other, the light shifting past me, flashing on his gold braid.

"Then tell me," I said. "What am I doing wrong? What am I forgetting?"

"The one who brought us here, you and I. That's what you're forgetting."

"Horn?" I asked.

"Give him to me." He bared his teeth. "Give me Horn and a cutlass and a minute to settle my score. Then I'll help you. Then I'll get you home."

"Damn you," I said.

"You're too late, boy." He laughed madly. "I'm damned already. I've nothing to lose."

I emptied his food from my bucket, spilling it on the deck. I left it where it lay, though he'd have to stretch his chains to the last link to reach it. Then I left him in the darkness and hurried to the deck.

Horn was steering. He kept the *Dragon*'s head just north of east, turning with the gusts, bearing up when they passed. It was a job that would strain almost any helmsman, but Horn kept at it in his mechanical way, as if he and the wind and the ship were one and the same.

"Don't you fret," he said. "Don't you worry, Mr Spencer. You've got a good head on your shoulders, and you'll figure out the sextant right enough."

"But the weather's changing," I said.

"Aye, it is." He turned the ship, and the wind plucked at his pigtail. "We'll have a ride before we're home." He smiled at me with the most disarming warmth. "It's good you've seen that, sir. You'll make a fine master, Mr Spencer. The type that's never short of crew."

"Thank you," I said, embarrassed. "But it was Grace who told me the weather was changing."

"The devil can tell that from down in the Cave?"

I nodded.

"What else did he say?"

It was on my lips to tell Horn about the bargain that Grace had offered: my friend's life for the safety of the ship. But I looked at him, so solid and strong, so good in his soul, and I kept my silence. I was frightened that he would go straight below and offer himself in trade.

"He thinks we'll all be drowned," I said. "He thinks we'll miss the Channel."

Horn scowled. "What do *you* think, Mr Spencer?"

"I think you were right, what you told me long ago."

"What was that?" he asked.

"There's no vessel as safe as the one that has old Horn aboard."

"Why, thank you, sir," he said.

I was surprised to see him blush. Then he coughed and turned his head away, and his hand went briefly to his cheek.

I stayed with him until the sun went down. We talked

about England — about London, really. All that Horn had seen of the city were the banks of the Thames and the roofs of the buildings that crowded around them. He asked about the streets and lanes, about palaces and parks, and I made myself homesick telling him about it. He longed to see it all himself, once his name was cleared and he could wander freely where he wanted, without a fear of press-gangs, or the hangman's noose that waited for deserters. He would walk through the city, he said: right through the city from one end to the other, then on to the west, through Reading and Marlborough, clear to the coast and his home near Bristol.

"I haven't been home in years," he said. "I wonder if it's changed."

The sky was nearly black, just speckling with stars. I stared up at the Big Dipper, and across at the wide wings of Cassiopeia. There, in those tiny lights, was all I needed to learn where we were and where we had to go. I took the sextant from its box again, and pointed it north to Polaris.

If I couldn't get a sight from the sun, I had little hope of doing it with the stars. But I shot Polaris seven times before the horizon disappeared and the black of the sea and the black of the sky became a single, solid sphere around us. Then I went below to my cabin, working away the hours on my bunk, until I fell asleep and dreamed of London.

I walked through the city again, from my father's office

to his docks on the Thames. But all the buildings were made of numbers, of towering fractions and vast façades of Roman numerals. And they trembled and tumbled down around me, and I woke to find Captain Butterfield shaking me by the shoulder.

My lamp was still burning, my bunk covered with books. Butterfield took his hand away and stood beside me. He wore his Sunday clothes, a dark suit that smelled of mothballs.

"Aren't you coming ashore?" he asked.

I felt almost dizzy with sleep.

"We're home," he said. "We're lying to the dock."

I had to drag myself from the ruins of the numbers onto a schooner leagues and leagues from England.

"Uncle Stanley," I said. "We're miles at sea."

"Nonsense," he said. "Feel the ship, son. Feel her." He stamped heavily on the deck. "You see?"

I sat upright. My lantern hung straight down from its hook, not moving at all. My ink bottle showed a level line of black. There was no sound of water, of wind. Butterfield stood so steady and straight that I wondered if he was right and I had slept away the voyage.

"Come along," he said.

I followed him from the cabin. A faint red light came down through the companionway, and I went up towards it and saw that dawn was breaking. The *Dragon* sat on a huge, flat sea. Not a ripple stirred the water. Not a breath of wind touched the sails. I had never seen a pond as calm as that. And it frightened me.

There was no one at the wheel. Horn and Dasher stood at the foremast, gazing up. Two other men smoked their pipes by the capstan, and I recognised them as Betts and Freeman.

Poor Uncle Stanley looked around, and his face fell. He had a glimpse, I thought, of the madness that the fever had brought him. He stood there in his fine wool suit, in his fancy shore-going shoes, as out of place as a pauper in a palace.

He blinked at me. "I heard it," he said. "The carriages and the crowds. I smelled the mud. The horses." He pressed his fingers against his temples. "What's wrong with me?" he asked.

If he *knew* he was mad, he *couldn't* be mad, I thought. "Sir," I said. "The sextant; it's bent."

"Is it?" he asked. "Who bent it, then?"

"Mudge," I said. "Remember? It fell from your locker."

"Yes," he said, with a look of terrible pain. "Yes, I do remember. It's off by three degrees."

"Which way?" I shook him. "Uncle, please. Which way?"

He had no chance to tell me. Horn came up from the waist. "I'd like to change to storm canvas," he said. "If you'll let me, sir." He seemed unsure of whom to ask, of who was now the master. "I'd like trysails fore and aft."

Butterfield rubbed his temples. "It's calm," he said. "Flat as a field."

"Not for long," said Horn. He pointed to the southwest, and I saw the clouds filling in. They were black and smoky, swirling at the edges. "Sir, please."

"Very well." Butterfield closed his eyes. "Do whatever you like."

He started away, but I grabbed his sleeve. "The sextant," I said.

He looked utterly bewildered.

"What do I do with the error?"

"Add," he said. "Add the error." He wandered away, going slowly towards his cabin.

I turned to Horn. "I'll help you with the topsail."

"No," he said. "I think that— Beg your pardon, sir. But I think you'd better take your sextant sights."

"It would be easier at noon," I said.

"You won't see the sun at noon." He glanced again to the southwest. "You won't see the sun again."

It was just what Grace had told me; somehow Grace had known just what the weather would bring. I watched Horn go forward, gathering what little crew he could muster. Then I went back to the sextant, though I loathed the thing. I stood by the rail to watch the sun come up, the redness bleeding from the sky. The *Dragon* never moved and never made a sound; her deck was steady as a wharf. I shot the sun as it peeked above the horizon, and again as it balanced on that hard, flat edge.

Its light was hot and bright; it blazed across the ocean. I took another pair of sights, then turned to go below. And

I saw the clouds building into towers, stretching out towards us. Horn was high above me, standing on a footrope that I couldn't quite see, as though he balanced on the clouds.

Chapter 26

Ploughing the Sea

I stood up from my bunk and stared at the chart. The marks I'd made, the little circles round my crosses, were bunched together like a clump of grapes. I stared at them and grinned. "There," I said softly. "*That's* where we be."

I snatched the chart from my bunk and carried it up to the deck. The *Dragon*, in her shrunken suit of heavy canvas, laboured before a hot and fitful wind. Hours had passed since dawn, and the sea that Butterfield had called a field was now a range of round-topped hills. We mounted each in turn, shuddering to the tops, lurching down the slopes. The sun was a pale dot in a whitened sky, with an enormous wheel of light around it, as though

God had marked it there as I had marked positions on my chart.

At the wheel stood Mudge, the farmer's son, the only man on deck. He glowered at the compass as it rocked and tilted in the gimbals. And he wrenched the wheel to port and then starboard, chasing the compass round its card.

"Don't stare at that," I said.

He whined, "There's nothing else to see."

"Then you're not looking," I said. "Steer by the wind or steer by the sea. If you give the ship her head, she'll look after herself better than that."

"I like to look at land," he said.

I shook my head. "Where's Horn? Where's Dasher?"

He raised his eyes for only a moment. "Up there."

I turned and looked aloft. Horn sat at the very masthead, high above the tiny topsail. Dasher was far below him, not twenty feet above the deck, clinging to the ratlines as if his life depended on it, his arms reaching past his bulging wineskins. He saw me and waved. Then he clamped his hand again to the rigging.

"Hello, John," he shouted. "Look, I'm aloft."

"What are you doing?" I said.

"We're inspecting the rig."

I smiled to myself. Horn must have told him that. *We'll inspect the rig*, he must have said, and Dasher had climbed as high as he'd dared, though what good he was doing I couldn't imagine.

"You can see the world from here." He talked at the top of his voice, but I could have heard him if he'd whispered. "Oh, it's grand to ride a tall ship when the sky is all you have for company." He motioned briefly through the air; his hand was shaking badly. "If it was stormy now, I'd be higher than the waves, wouldn't I, John?"

"Indeed," I said.

"Think of it!" he cried. "There's nothing to hold me up but a bit of rope, and we're miles and miles and miles from land."

"A hundred and eighty," I said.

"Think of that, my friend."

And he must have thought of it, for he plucked briefly at the worn ratlines and scrambled down as quickly as a spider. He was out of breath, his face as red as his coat.

Horn came behind him, swinging out from the mast into nothing but air. He slid down the lift to the tip of the yard, down the edge of the sail with only his fingers and thumbs to hold him, down the sheet to the deck: a long, long slide that made my stomach churn, though I had little fear of being aloft.

Even Dasher must have seen how it made his own adventures pale. But Horn clapped a hand on his shoulder hard enough to set the wineskins bouncing. "Good for you," he said. "You'll be a topman any day."

"I only wish the mast was higher," said Dasher. It seemed he almost meant it. But then, Horn had a way of inspiring everyone.

And I thought with a pang of guilt that Horn wouldn't have snapped at Mudge as I had done; he would have shown him how to steer.

Horn's hand sat on Dasher's shoulder like a big, brown animal. He looked at me, at the chart in my hand. "Have you done it?" he asked.

I wanted to hear his praise. I knelt on the deck and spread the chart open. I pointed at the little crowd of marks I'd made.

Dasher stooped beside me. "You did it?" he asked.

"Yes. We're here," I said. "Or at sunrise we were here. I'll stream the log and see how far we've gone, but it's pretty close."

I looked up at Horn. He peered at the chart and at the sea, as though he knew the oceans so well that he could judge if I was right. He said, "Then we're too far to the north. We have to harden the sheets."

It was all he said. He went forward to trim the sails, and he took Dasher with him. I was left by myself, my finger still touching the chart, a lump in my throat. He had praised Dasher for climbing a scant twenty feet into the rigging, but he hadn't even thanked me for finding our position.

I rolled the chart and took it aft; I stuffed it into the holder at the side of the binnacle. I took the log and the sandglass from their drawer. Mudge still steered by the compass, weaving us up and down the swells, sweating from his unnecessary labours.

"Bring us round to sou'east," I said.

He flung the wheel hard over.

"Not like that!" I said. "Easy with it, man."

He blinked stupidly, the look of a dog told to do something it didn't understand.

"Here." I shoved him aside and took the wheel. The spokes were slick with his sweat. I sighed. "Look, you can *feel* her," I said. "She wants to come into the wind; she'll always come into the wind if you let her. So you give her a touch whenever she turns."

"To remind her, like," said Mudge.

I shrugged.

"Like you're driving a plough horse."

I'd never done that; I didn't know.

"You have to think ahead of her."

"Yes," I said. "Something like that."

I gave him back the wheel and went aft with the log. I lowered it over the rail, into a wake that twisted and turned as wildly as it ever had with Mudge at the helm. But I'd done my best, I thought; I'd tried. And I turned the glass over to start the sand flowing through it, and let the line stream out astern.

The seas rose high above me, their round tops only now beginning to break. The stern rose above them, then dipped so low that the log line stretched above me, bent in a bow by the wind. I watched the sand trickle down through the glass, the line going slowly from its reel, then faster as we mounted a crest and slid to the trough. When the glass was empty, I gathered in the line, counting the knots to gauge our speed. Then I looked back at the wake; it stretched nearly straight behind us.

I worked my figures as I walked back to the wheel. Our speed times the hours: we'd gone thirty miles since dawn.

Mudge was smiling. He steered with one hand, pushing down on the wheel as the *Dragon* soared over the swells.

"I've got it now," he said. Pride was all over his face. "I'm ploughing the sea, Mr Spencer. And behind us, that's my furrow."

"Well, good for you," I said, trying to sound like Horn. "Good for you, Mr Mudge."

"How far do we have to go?" he asked.

"A hundred and fifty miles," I said. "We should sight England in the morning watch."

My prediction spread through the ship; our whole little crew knew it by sunset. Even Butterfield understood, when I went to his cabin to tell him.

"In the morning?" he said. "That's splendid." He was sitting in his chair, still in his Sunday clothes. "Put a lookout on the bow," he said. "I'll give a guinea to the man who first sights land."

"We haven't men to spare," I said.

He fiddled with his tight collar. "But, John," he said. "What if we come on the land in the night? Surely it's only sensible."

It pleased me to see he was right, and morning — I

hoped — would find him back to his old self. We divided the crew into watches of two men apiece, and I stood the first myself, steering the ship as Dasher sat at the bow.

The wind continued to rise, and we fled to the east before the gathering storm. I felt the force of it high in the topsail; I heard it coming in a whine of rigging, like the voices of the buccaneers. It chased us towards England.

By the end of my watch, there were thirty knots of wind aloft, and it was backing steadily to the south. Spindrift blew over the stern, and waves broke over the bow. Both Dasher and I were soaked to the skin when Mudge came to take my place, and Freeman sent Dasher below.

Mudge braced his feet. He spat on his hands and grabbed the wheel.

"Can you handle her?" I asked.

"Aye, sir," he said. "I think so, sir."

He leaned his considerable weight on the leeward spokes and shouted at the ship as he might at a horse. "Haw!" he yelled, letting the wheel come up, and "Gee!" as he bore it down. He was a strong helmsman, if a wild one, and I saw we were safe in his hands.

I watched the masts tilt and straighten, the guns snub up at their lashings. Horn had dressed the ship in a suit of small sails, and I was sure she could handle whatever the weather would bring. So I nodded to Mudge and went below, feeling content and free of worries.

I put on the driest clothes I had and sat happily to a

meal of cold fish and damp bread. The pots swung on their hooks; the kettle rattled and the gimballed lamp stood on its side. Out of the shadows came Butterfield. Leaning with the ship, he balanced at the same angle as the lamp, as though some strange power held him slanted on the deck.

My hopes that his fever had broken vanished at the sight of him. Sad and drawn, he walked past the table without a word, then touched the porthole, turned, and left again. I spoke to him, but he didn't answer. As long as I sat there, he wandered through the ship like a lost soul, in and out of his cabin, up to the deck and back below, with his Sunday suit dripping salt water. It made me think of the day my mother died and how he'd come to the house, fresh from the sea in those very same clothes. He'd walked from room to room, as silent then as now, his lips moving in conversations from years ago with a woman who no longer lived.

On his third trip through the galley I rose and took his elbow. I steered him to his cabin, and if he was even aware that I was there, then it wasn't me he walked with. He started talking, suddenly, about his days in Father's office. But when I settled him down, he fell asleep in a moment. "We're almost home," I said. "You'll be better once we're home."

I took a bit of bread to Captain Grace, and tossed it in through the door, as a zookeeper would. He had to scramble to catch it as it tumbled down the deck. His chains jerked taut at his ankles. "Is that all you'll bring me?" he asked.

I had no pity for him. I blamed everything on Grace: my uncle's pitiful state; the death of Abbey; even the storm that chased us home. It was all his fault in my mind.

"I need water," he said.

Already I was closing the door. "This time tomorrow we'll be in the Channel," I said. "And soon enough you'll have all the bread and water that you like, when you're locked in the hulks at Chatham."

Then at last I went to sleep. The sounds of the ship and the sea dissolved into a steady drone. The last things I heard were the latch on the captain's door and the steady tapping of Uncle's Sunday shoes as he wandered up and down the passageway.

For hours I slept, right through the watch and well into Horn's. But I knew he was steering when I dragged myself out of my bunk, for the *Dragon* slithered through the waves in an easy, rolling motion. Only Horn could do that when the seas were like this: wild enough that I had to stand with one foot on the deck and one on the wall.

The door crashed open when I touched it. I pulled myself through and staggered down the passageway. I heard fists bashing at the door to the Cave, but I didn't bother to look. I hauled myself up to the deck as a cold rush of water tumbled down on my shoulders. Then I climbed over the coaming and stared into the darkness at Horn.

He sat on the deck, his back to the binnacle. And towering behind him was Bartholomew Grace.

Chapter 27

A Deadly Struggle

"Stay there!" shouted Grace. "Come no closer, I tell you."

He stood at the wheel as the sea raged behind him, his hair and his coat streaming forward in the wind. At his feet was Horn — half sitting, half crouched on the deck — his back rigid against the binnacle. He was tied to it, I saw, held there by his key string. If he moved from the binnacle, if he slipped on the deck, he would strangle on that bit of twine.

I looked for the other man on watch, but the night was too dark to see very clearly. I wondered if I could tackle Grace by myself.

As he had before, he seemed to know my thoughts. He

reached into his coat and pulled out a flintlock. He aimed it, not at me, but at Horn. "If you take another step," he said. "I shall send him to his Maker."

It was the double-barrelled gun from Butterfield's cabin, hung from a lanyard now at the pirate's neck.

"What have you done to the captain?" I asked, shouting into the wind.

"Why, nothing," said he. "Kindness is as kindness does, my son."

How I hated to hear that word from his lips. "Where is he, then?"

"In that fine little cabin that you appointed for my use. All the comforts that you gave me now are his."

The noise I had heard — the bashing — it must have been Butterfield. "And the lookout?" I asked.

"Ah," said Grace. "Well, he wasn't as kind."

"He killed him," said Horn.

Grace smiled, if such a wicked look could be called a smile. "Kindness is as kindness does, my son."

I lowered my head as a blast of spindrift flew over the stern. The *Dragon* pitched forward and Horn slid away from the binnacle. He grasped at his string, hanging from it until he braced his feet again.

"What do you want?" I said.

The awful, melted face was looking down at Horn, studying his agony. "Well, I want you to go forward," he said. "I want you to turn out the crew and wear ship."

"In this weather?" I said. "You'll dismast her."

"And I want you not to argue," said Grace.

"But the mast," I said. "Can't you feel how it shakes?"

He stepped to the side of the wheel. With a kick, he swept Horn's feet away and let him dangle on the tightened string. He grabbed the twine where it looped around the binnacle and gave it a turn with his fist. Horn groaned as it cut at his throat.

"Stop!" I cried. "I'll do it. Whatever you say, I'll do it."

"Everyone comes up by the fo'c's'le," said Grace. "First you and then the others."

The *Dragon* ran at a terrible speed. I went forward through a waist that slopped with water, up to the foredeck, then down through the hatch. The lantern glowed dimly below, its light absorbed by sodden, torn socks hanging there. I turned up the flame, then woke Dasher and Mudge, Freeman and Betts. I told them that Grace had taken the ship.

"Why?" asked Dasher, climbing from his hammock. He had slept in his coat and wineskins, but not in his boots. "What does he mean to do with it?"

"I don't know," I said.

"We're going back to Culebra, I'd bet." He wedged himself down by Horn's chest. His boots were stuffed behind it, and he pulled on one, over a sock so often darned that it was nothing but patches. "He's going after my barrel, the devil."

"He's got Horn tied to the binnacle," I said.

Dasher looked up. "He overpowered Horn?"

"Yes," I said.

"Lord love me." His face was pale as snow. "He got the better of Horn?"

"And he has a pistol," I said. "The only one on the ship."

"Well, not quite the only one," said Dasher. He brought out his other boot and turned it upside down. Onto the deck tumbled the most sinister thing I'd ever seen, a tiny pistol set atop a short and wicked blade. Dasher passed it up to me.

The blade was rusted and dull, the tip broken away. I saw why Dasher's socks were in the state they were. "It's been in your boot all this time?" I asked.

Dasher nodded. The blade was speckled with rust, the flintlock frozen shut. I tried to pull it back, and Dasher winced.

"Is it loaded?" I asked.

"Lord, no," said Dasher. None of his pistols were ever loaded. "I'm afraid you'll break the hammer off, that's all."

Flakes of rust came away in my hand. The gun hadn't been cocked in years, if ever. But Grace wouldn't know that. I shoved it into my belt, below the tails of my shirt, and shook Mudge from his hammock. Freeman and Betts were already up, but both were still so sick with the fever that they could only stand by holding on to each other.

"Can you get to the deck?" I asked them.

They nodded, their teeth chattering. I wanted Grace to

see them, to know for himself that he hadn't men enough to work the ship.

"Follow me," I said.

We went aft in a straggling line, hunched against the wind and spray, finding handholds where we could. The *Dragon* thundered on, far faster than when I'd last calculated her speed. The hours that I'd thought we'd take to fetch the land were shrinking quickly.

She corkscrewed down a wave, and I darted through the waist with Dasher clinging to my arm. Mudge lumbered behind us, and poor Freeman and Betts lagged far behind, hobbling along as waves roared over the rail and buried them waist-deep in water. But we climbed to the quarterdeck and stood before Grace, as pitiful a crew as ever had been assembled.

"Get aloft," he said. "I want the topsail furled."

"We can't," I told him. "Look for yourself."

He stretched his hand towards the noose at Horn's neck, and I had no doubt that he would twist the life out of him.

"Don't," I cried. "We'll clew it up to the yard. Isn't that enough?"

"You'll go aloft." He pointed at me, at Dasher, at Mudge. "You and you and you."

"Dasher?" I said.

"He's a topman, isn't he?"

I groaned inside. It was just like Dasher to have told a tale like that. Beside me he quivered, his eyes gazing up at the mainmast as it reeled through a blackness streaked with grey. Dawn was coming to our wasteland of water.

"Now," said Grace. He shoved his pistol at Freeman, then Betts. "You two. Cast off the sheets."

We went forward in a little group, up the weather side. The cannons strained at their lashing, their wooden wheels squeaking. Mudge started up the ratlines with a steady mindlessness that I envied. The mast swung so far and so quickly that I dreaded climbing to a yard that would tilt in every direction.

But if I was scared, Dasher — above me — was terrified. He stepped up to the rail, and his boots slipped away on the wet wood. Only the wind kept him from falling. It plastered his coat against the ratlines and glued him to the rigging. He could barely move his arms for the bulk of his wineskins.

"I can't go up there," he said.

"You've done it before," I told him. On the *Dragon's* first voyage, Dasher had climbed right to the masthead to watch for a ship in the fog.

"But not in weather like this." He looked down, his face wretched with fear. "Not with the mast breaking off. And not in these wineskins; I can't move in these bladders."

"Take them off," I said.

"No chance!" he shouted.

"Then climb."

He stretched out an arm, then a leg, and dragged

himself up like a huge, red bat. A step; another. The *Dragon* fell from a wave, and his coat billowed past his shoulders. "John," he said. "John, I can't do it."

Mudge was up at the crosstrees, hurtling round and round as the mast carved circles from the night. He looked down at me, I up at him, and Dasher was between us, frozen to the shrouds.

A loud crack nearly startled the life from me, and the night glowed briefly, faintly, from the flash of Grace's gun.

"He's shooting at us," I said. "Dasher, can't you move?"

"No," said Dasher. He was crying. His head on the ratlines, his arms spread wide, he shook and sobbed, and his silly wineskins pulsed like lungs. "Help," he said. "John, please help me."

"Stay where you are." I reached up to pat his boot, then climbed down to the rail, to the deck. I went past the cannons, up towards the wheel. I drew Dasher's pistol from my belt.

"Get aloft!" shouted Grace. He pointed the flintlock right at me, then down at Horn. One shot was left. "I'll blow his brains out if you don't."

A wave battered on the stern. Spray flew up from either quarter, and the *Dragon* lurched to starboard. Horn fell away from the binnacle, his hands reaching up for the string. The *dragon* heeled farther, until the deck sloped away from me, down to the wheel and Bartholomew Grace.

His knee was bent, his arm pressing on the spokes to

bring the *Dragon* upright. Horn flailed at his feet, kicking for a hold on the deck, and the sea bubbled and churned at the rail. Grace glanced towards it, and I leapt down the deck.

I flew at him, screaming at the top of my voice. He looked up, and the flintlock rose in his hand. I crashed into him as the *Dragon* settled in her roll, as the seas roared onto the deck. The gun fired wildly, and Grace tumbled backwards, vanishing into the water that filled the deck.

I grabbed the binnacle. Horn was hanging from his key string, his legs kicking, his hands grabbing frantically at his throat. With the blade on my pistol I hacked through the twine, and Horn slid feet first down the slanted deck, plunging into the same wave that had swallowed Bartholomew Grace.

The *Dragon* broached. Another wave followed the last, and the topsail boomed in the blackness with a thunder that shook the hull. I hauled at the wheel, but the *Dragon* felt heavy and dead, as though she had drowned in those terrible seas. Slowly she shifted, and climbed from the waves. And the sea spilled from her decks in a churning foam.

Then up from the water stood Bartholomew Grace.

He glared at me with his dead man's face as the water tumbled round his waist. He hadn't far to come, and he took a step towards me. The pistol was still in his hand, the lanyard stretched tight to his neck. He took another step, then staggered and started clubbing at the water, raising little spouts and splashes. Then the sea went surging off the deck, and there was Horn, no longer tied, clutching at the pirate's coat.

They tumbled down together and rose together, locked in a deadly struggle as the sea surged up around them. Grace twisted his fist in the collar of Horn's shirt; Horn clawed at the flintlock, then at its lanyard, and hauled himself up to the buccaneer's throat.

They swayed and tilted, reeled and turned. They battled down the deck as the *Dragon* hurtled on. She bashed through a wave and into another. Spray flew up in the sheets.

Horn was bigger and stronger than Grace. His enormous arms bent and lifted the pirate clear off the deck. But Grace never let go of the shirt collar, and the pair went spinning down towards the rail. They hit against it chest to chest and wrestled there, each choking the life from the other. For a moment Horn was looking at me. Then he shouted, and his arms went stiff as boards. He held on to Grace with all the strength he had, and flung himself over the rail. They fell together into the sea; together they went, off the edge of our wooden world.

"Horn!" I screamed. "Horn!"

But he was gone, and there was no hope of trying to find him. The *Dragon* hurtled on, from wave to wave in a spindrift shroud. She reeled and shook, the topsail banged and clattered, and I looked up to see Mudge, a black spot high in the rigging, making his way up the topmast shrouds, going doggedly on to reef that sail. Dasher still clung to the ratlines, and I saw what little time had passed since I'd started aft to end all this. Now Grace was gone, and Horn with him, and I imagined the two of them sinking slowly through the ocean, tumbling down through fathom after fathom, embraced for all eternity.

I stood by the wheel and stared at a ragged scar on the deck, a hole ringed by splinters to show where Grace's pistol had fired. But I couldn't dwell on it, or grieve for Horn. I heard a voice wailing faintly over the wind and the sea. Mudge was pointing forwards.

"Land!" he was shouting.

The *Dragon* rose to a crest and I saw it myself, beyond the endless rows of whitecapped waves. A smudge of the earth, a line of cliffs dark in the dawn, lay directly before us. It vanished as the *Dragon* surfed to the trough, then appeared again. Within the hour we'd be right below them. And we couldn't turn away with the topsail set.

I shouted for Dasher to take the wheel. I called as loudly as I could. But if he heard me, he misunderstood, for he started aloft then, inching up the ratlines in a swirl of crimson. He reached the crosstrees and squeezed through the lubber's hole, and the wind seemed to squirt him through it as his coat billowed above him.

Mudge waited for him, and helped him up to the yard. They stepped out to leeward on a sagging rope, high above the deck, then high above the sea, as the *Dragon* rolled along. Betts cast off the sheet, Freeman the clew, and half the sail went streaming out. The men aloft gathered it in.

My heart was up there with Dasher. I knew how frightening it could be to balance on a thread of rope and grab at canvas that tried its best to pull me off. I had never done it in weather as bad as this, on a mast that pitched so wildly. But Mudge — as thick as a loaf when he worked on deck — was spry and nimble aloft. He dragged the sail into the yard, and Dasher tied the gaskets round it.

The cliffs grew higher, darker, swifter in their coming. I saw the surf at their feet, a strip of green at their tops.

When the topsail was furled, I turned the wheel. The *Dragon* flew along with the shore on her beam. And a spit of land came out to meet us.

It blocked us like a wall, a tremendous hurdle that we couldn't cross. Wreathed with surf and spray, it was a jagged finger pointing south. I knew it at once as the Northground Cape.

In the past two years I had witnessed a shipwreck and a smuggling run, a voyage to the Indies. And it had all brought me back to the very same place where I'd started, to St Elmo's Bay and the teeth of the Tombstones.

Chapter 28

The Wreck

We wore ship and beat our way west. The tiny storm sails thrummed with the wind as the *Dragon* clawed against it. I watched the land go by, the places that I knew. There were Sugar Bay and Tobacco Cove; every nook had a name that remembered a shipwreck and the cargo that drifted ashore.

I saw the cliffs where the wreckers had lit false beacons, and the whitened fury of the sea where it broke against the Tombstones. There lay the wreck of the *Isle of Skye*, my father's finest ship, her bones still resting among those of many others. Then Wrinkle Head was off the bow, a wall as steep as the Northground. And again we turned to bash our way east, trapped between the capes.

Butterfield had been tossed about his dark prison so badly that he was a mass of bruises. "He's black and blue from end to end," said Mudge, who had found him fainted in the Cave and had carried him to the after cabin. "He's in a very bad way, I think."

Betts and Freeman had gone back to their hammocks, their chills worsened by the night. Only Dasher and Mudge and I were left to work the *Dragon*, and we beat back and forth across St Elmo's Bay as the wind howled from the south.

The waves that had pushed the *Dragon* on, that had slipped for miles and miles beneath her stern, now came tumbling towards her sides. They shattered on her planks in great booms and blasts of spray, or thundered right aboard to fill the waist from rail to rail. We rolled like a log in troughs so deep that the water there was streaked with sand. And on the starboard tacks, the topmast shook worse than ever, with an awful rattle in the rigging.

Now I held her head up on the larboard tack as we bounded west towards Wrinkle Head. If we could round it, we were safe; the harbour of Pendennis lay just beyond the cape. But to round it, we had to pass the Tombstones.

Mudge had heard of them. So had Freeman and Betts; there wasn't a sailor in England who didn't fear those jagged rocks. But Dasher didn't know them, and he gazed at the enormous spouts of water tossed up by breaking waves.

He was full of himself now, after his trip aloft.

"Speaking as a topman," he said, "I don't care for this at all. I've been aloft, John, and I'll vouch for this: you don't want to take a ship in there."

I didn't tell him that I'd done so before, that it was I who had watched the false lights and shouted orders to the helmsman, that it was I who had guided the lovely *Isle of Skye* straight towards her doom.

"But the water's flat behind them," Dasher said. "I could see that from the yard, John. We who work among the birds can spot things from aloft." Then he looked up at the topsail yard, and his courage seemed to leave him. "Lord love me. That thing's working loose."

He was right, but only by half. The yard swung side to side, though the braces were tight. It was the topmast itself that was close to breaking.

"When you inspected the rig," I asked, "what did you find?"

Dasher frowned. "The cuff?" he said. "No, that's not right. The *collar*. I didn't go clear to the masthead, mind; I didn't see it for myself. But Horn said the collar was cracked."

It was all that held the mast up. The shrouds were shackled to that metal ring. If the collar broke, the mast would go.

I steered for the end of Wrinkle Head, into the wind and the seas, into a current that swept us north. The waves broke on the point in a mournful drum, and I knew we'd never round it.

I looked at the Tombstones coming closer, at the cliffs behind them, where I'd once climbed from the beach to escape the wreckers. At the top were people, dark figures that hadn't been there earlier. Women and children and men, they gathered along the cliffs' edge like crows flocking to a rooftop.

Dasher waved. "They've come to watch us pass," he said.

I shook my head. "They've come to see the wreck."

They'd come from Pendennis, up to the moor and south to the sea. They'd come as they'd done for decades, to watch a tiny ship struggle against the enormous sea, to watch her lose in the end. They'd be wondering now what she carried, a ship as small as this, and what fine things would wash ashore when the wind and the seas overcame her.

"Ready about," I said.

Dasher and Mudge went forward to tend our little jib. I turned the wheel and the *Dragon* swung into the seas, round through the south. The sails emptied and flogged, then filled again, and we tacked to the east as all of Pendennis followed on the cliffs above us.

We sailed right to the Northground Cape, fighting for a bit of sea room. But the waves pushed us back, and the wind moaned in the rigging, and we were no farther from shore when I shouted again, "Ready about."

The *Dragon* heeled up to the wind, and for a moment it seemed that she wouldn't turn. She hung there with her sails shaking, the waves sweeping over the bowsprit. She came to a dead stop, and the crowd on the cliffs pressed closer to the edge. In a moment she would start to drift backwards; in another she'd be into the surf. But a crested wave hammered on the bow and gave her the mere little push that she needed, and back we went to the west: the ship; her crew; the people on the shore.

We needed more sail, but we hadn't men enough to set it. We could only hope that the wind would change before the topmast broke, that it might ease enough to let us round the point. We could only hope for a bit of luck. But it seemed we'd had none of that since Horn had gone over the side.

I steered the *Dragon* west again as the topmast shook and bent. Wrinkle Head came closer. The waves rolled below us, then on towards the shore. They shattered on the Tombstones, and the spray soared up to the tops of the cliffs, to the people waiting there.

"A boat!" cried Dasher. He shook my arm and pointed.

I saw it too, a tiny thing tilting over a crest. Rowed by a man and a boy, it staggered through the waves, coming east around the point. The boy, in a black sou'wester, rowed for all he was worth, then stopped to bail the boat. The man was huge; he worked his little craft through the waves and surf, and the current bore him on.

"Bless their hearts," said Dasher. "They've come to help us."

"Help us wreck," said Mudge. "They'll slit our throats

and steer the ship ashore, and who's to tell it happened? Not those vultures on the cliff."

"It's not like that," I said. "Not any more. Not here, at least."

But Mudge would never be convinced. He feared the wreckers more than the Tombstones, and he begged me to turn the ship around.

"They'll kill us," he said.

But I kept my course. For all my life I'd wanted to be a seaman, and from childhood it had been my wildest dream to sail a ship that I commanded, to take her far and bring her home again. And now I *was* a captain, though on a ship with a toppling mast and a usable crew of only two, with a storm-tossed shore so close at hand that I could almost spit upon the cliffs. But I made my decision, and I kept my course.

The *Dragon* shouldered into enormous waves and shook from her trembling mast. The little rowing boat burst through a plume of froth two crests away, and the man turned towards me as he skidded to the trough.

"It's Simon Mawgan," I said.

"Mawgan!" shouted Mudge. "The Mawgans are the worst of them."

"Not any more," I said. That I was still alive was due in part to Simon Mawgan.

He was a powerful rower. He turned the little boat so that he'd meet the *Dragon* as she passed, and the boy rowed with him, stroke for stroke. But the boat was heavy, and the seas swept over it, bow to stern. The boy shipped his oars and bailed; he bailed by the bucket as the water rushed in by the gallon.

"Just who needs saving here?" asked Dasher.

"Take the line when they come alongside," I told him. "Mudge, you cast off the sheets when I luff."

"Luff?" he said. "Don't. Not here."

"Go," I told him.

The boat skittered across our path. I turned the *Dragon* up to the wind, and the jib snapped and flogged as the sheets came loose. Mawgan's boat — above me one moment, below me the next — came flitting from crest to crest as the waves slopped over the rail. The boy held a coil of line, and Dasher was ready to catch it. But the boat rocked and skidded sideways, and the *Dragon* heeled towards it. Mawgan backed his oars; then I lost sight of his boat past the curve of the deck. I was certain that we'd crush it under the hull. But again he rose beside me, rowing furiously ahead, and the next wave picked up the boat by the stern and swept it over the rail. Mudge hardened the sheets, and the *Dragon* bore off to the east, and there the boat sat as the water fell away, flat on its keel on our deck.

I would never have planned to do that; I couldn't have managed it if I'd tried. Even Mawgan was taken by surprise, and he sat in the boat with the oars in his hands. He gazed around, wide-eyed, as though he'd been dropped suddenly from the stars. Then he saw me at the wheel.

"By the saints!" he cried. "John Spencer!"

The boy turned his head. He took off his sou'wester, and I saw it wasn't a boy at all. It was Mary, Simon's niece. She leapt from the boat and ran to meet me. We hugged each other as the *Dragon* raced along.

Dasher laughed. "If I'd known the fishing was like this, I'd have brought a net," he said.

Mary was wet as a sponge, but I didn't care. She was two years older than last I'd seen her, and even prettier than before. I squeezed the water from her, and could have stood like that for ever, I thought. But Mawgan stamped up from the waist, and the *Dragon* rolled the water from his little boat. I saw a long cable coiled in its bottom, the fluke of an anchor reaching out.

"You were coming to Pendennis," said Mary. Her lovely Cornish accent hadn't changed. "You were coming to see me. Edn't it true?"

"'Course he wasn't," bellowed Mawgan. "He lost his way. He's got a topmast near to breaking, and he can't round the point for the weather."

Mary gazed up at me.

"Yes," I said. "We lost our way."

"Where are your men?" Mawgan shouted. "Where's the rest of the crew?"

"We're all that's left," I said. "We've had fever and gunfights and storms. The ship was taken, and taken back again. The captain's down below, and there are two hands in the fo'c'sle, and we're all that's left — Dasher and Mudge and I."

"Yet you kept her afloat?" Mawgan smiled. "You've done well, for a Londoner. Now let's get you safe and sound."

He pulled Mary away. We wore ship and headed west, punching through the waves. He put Dasher and Mudge to work, and the cable was uncoiled from his boat. It was led forward, outboard of the shrouds, and bent to the capstan. Then the anchor was hauled from the boat to the rail, and Mawgan came back to the wheel.

"Steer for the Tombstones," he said.

I could scarcely believe I'd heard him right. "The Tombstones?" I asked.

He nodded. "Can you see them?" he said. "'Course you can. A blind man would know they were there."

It was true enough. The surf on the Tombstones was a heavy, muffled thunder, the sound of a thousand guns in a broadside that never ended. I turned the ship towards it.

The seas grew bigger and steeper. They pitched us forward and went rumbling on to break their backs on the spikes of rock.

"Closer," Mawgan said. "Closer still. You want to nearly touch them, John."

All of Pendennis watched us from the cliffs beyond the Tombstones. It was the hardest thing I'd ever done to point the *Dragon* at that wild white water. I lived all over again the horrors of the *Isle of Skye* as the thunder of the Tombstones grew loud enough to shake the air. I watched the bowsprit rise and fall, the spouts shoot up and whirlpools open. I saw Dasher, in the waist, tighten the cords on his wineskins, and Mudge look up with fear in his eyes. Even Mary seemed frightened; she had seen many wrecks in her life.

But Mawgan might have been sailing down the Thames for all the concern he showed. He held on to the binnacle with one hand, staring around at the sea and the shore. I was nearly maddened by his nonchalance, until I saw his fingers. They were white, and locked like talons on the wood.

Then the breakers were all around us. The *Dragon* heaved herself towards the rocks, and heaved herself away. The spray and the spume made a fog that was thick as wool. We went tearing through it, into a blinding whiteness, and that roaring filled my ears. A rock rose up, seething with foam; it stood square before the bowsprit.

"Left!" shouted Mawgan. He pushed on the spokes. The *Dragon* wove between the breakers. She tilted nearly onto her side; the topsail yard touched the sea, and a shroud parted with a crack.

"Now right!" cried Mawgan. Again we turned the wheel.

The broken shroud tumbled down, snaking in the wind. It tangled in the trysail sheets and drummed against the guns. The mast bent like a feather, then straightened as the starboard shrouds went taut. The waves battered at us, and Mawgan cried, "Let the anchor go!"

Mudge heaved it over the rail. Fifty pounds of iron

tumbled over the side, and the cable bounded after it. I felt a tug as it touched the bottom, another when it bounced. *Hold*, I thought. But we dragged the anchor on, out from the fog of spindrift, towards the cliffs and the beach below them.

Then the anchor caught. The wheel was snatched from my hands, and the *Dragon* rounded up with a dizzying speed. Every timber creaking, the cable so taut that it crackled, the *Dragon* settled head to wind in a circle of calm in the lee of the Tombstones. And there she stopped, amid blankets of writhing kelp, barely twice her length from the beach.

The waves rolled in, broke along their tops, shattered into spray and froth. But they reached us tamed to a gentle swell that was flattened by the kelp. And among the dark shapes of the Tombstones hung a score of rainbows that shimmered in the spindrift.

Mawgan clapped me on the back. "Well done," he said. Then Mary came up to the wheel, Mudge and Dasher too, and we stood together watching the rainbows form and disappear. It seemed impossible that we'd sailed through there.

"I didn't think the anchor would stick in the sand," I said.

"It didn't," said Mawgan. "We hooked onto the wreck."

"What wreck?"

"The *Isle of Skye*."

I felt a shiver, a prickly twinge in my spine. The wreck

that had once nearly taken my life had now saved it, as though a great and mysterious circle had been completed. When I was washed from that beautiful brig, I'd been a landsman, and now I clung to her bones as a sailor, as the captain of another ship. What a long way I had gone to get back to where I had started!

We would wait there, swinging over the drowned ribs of the *Isle of Skye*, for a fair wind to blow us home to London. My uncle Stanley would recover from the fever, as would Freeman and Betts. Dasher would slip away to his home in Kent, and one day — I was sure — would sail back to the West Indies to find his barrel of silver. I would think often of Horn and his chest of doomed vessels, for his bottles would travel with me over the years, from ship to ship.

I stood beside Mary and wondered if she might join me, if we might not voyage together to all the oceans of the world. It was on my lips to ask her that. But she spoke before me.

"John," she said. "Will you come home to Galilee?"

I thought of her house beyond the cliffs, her garden of flowers that remembered old wrecks and people that she'd known. I thought of the stable, of the pony she rode wildly on the moor. And I saw that while I had changed, she had not. Mary was a match for any oarsman, but she was as rooted in the Cornish soil as the flowers she tended. And she could no more leave the land than I could settle on it.

She sighed and leaned her head against me. "You have

to stay with the ship," she said. "Edn't that the way it is?"

"Yes," I said. We had to furl the sails and fit new shrouds; we had a hundred things to do. That would always be the way it was.

Mary smiled. "You can't stay, can you, John Spencer?"

"No," I said. "But one day I'll be back."

And I meant it then. I meant it with all my heart.

Author's Note

This story takes place in the early months of 1803, long after the last of the great buccaneers had been swept from the seas. When the *Dragon* set sail for the Indies, Henry Morgan had been dead for 115 years, Blackbeard for 85. Captain Kidd had gone to the gallows in 1701, swearing to the end that he had done nothing wrong. "I am the innocentest person of them all," he told the judge who sentenced him to death.

Kidd might have been a butcher of English grammar, but he was scarcely the terror of the seven seas that legend has portrayed him to be. Born in Scotland, made rich in New York through marriage and business, Kidd returned to Britain in the late 1600s, seeking command of a king's privateer. Instead, he fell among a group of politicians, all earls and lords and dukes. They agreed to fit him out with his own ship for a voyage to the Indian Ocean, where he might privateer against the French and plunder the pirate ships that were themselves plundering English merchantmen. King William III gave his personal blessing to the plan.

Kidd sailed first to New York, then east around the Cape of Storms. His crew was picked away by press-gangs and disease and replaced by desperate men who were promised a share of each prize. But when the riches weren't quick in coming, the crew rose against the captain. Despite his problems, Kid tried to stay within the shady laws that protected him. He flew a French flag to board the merchantman *Quedagh Merchant*, tricking her captain into producing the French pass that was all Kidd needed to claim her as a rightful prize. Kidd abandoned his own ship — by then leaking and rotten — and sailed off in the *Quedagh Merchant*.

In 1699, less than three years after leaving England, Kidd arrived in the West Indies, where he learned that the English government had branded him a pirate. In desperation, he sailed north to Hispaniola and anchored in a lonely cove. A pirate trader came to buy the scraps of cargo that remained on the *Quedagh Merchant* and bought the ship as well. Kidd purchased a sloop, loaded aboard a few chests of gold, and headed home to New York, hoping to clear his name or buy his freedom. Instead, he was arrested for piracy and shipped to England for trial.

The French pass from the *Quedagh Merchant* might have saved him, but it mysteriously went missing. Kidd hinted at his agreement with the politicians and the king, but he remained loyal to his employers and was hanged for his silence. The rope broke; he was hanged again, and then his body was tarred and suspended in chains.

The gold Kidd took with him to New York was recovered from the various places where he had hidden it. Together it amounted to £14,000, a tiny fraction of the then staggering fortune of £400,000 that rumour said he'd collected during his voyage. There was so much treasure unaccounted for that careers were made in searching for it through the centuries that followed. Even President Franklin Roosevelt took a stab at treasure hunting. But nothing more was ever found.

It became a legend that Kidd had buried his treasure on the eastern shore of North America. Somewhere between the Indies and Canada, it seemed, he had anchored his sloop, landed with all his chests and his riches, and buried them deep in the earth.

But what if he hid the treasure *before* he left for New York, before he even reached Hispaniola? What if he found an island with an empty harbour on his way through the Caribbean? What if he stopped at Culebra?

The island was right in his path. Its pattern of hills, its twisting shoreline with one good harbour, come surprisingly close to the Treasure Island described by Robert Louis Stevenson. If there is a buried treasure yet to be found, could it possibly lie in Culebra?

Bartholomew Grace believed it did, but Grace is a fictional character. He was created from the necessity of having a buccaneer in a time when there were no buccaneers. The West Indies of 1803, as attested by John Spencer's father — and maintained by Roland Abbey — were haunted by cut-throats who attacked passing ships from their bases onshore in swarms of little boats. Grace had to be more than that, and worse than that. His career is based on the sad tale of John Rodney, the son of the great British admiral George Rodney. John went to sea as a midshipman at the age of fifteen, and it took him less than a week to be made a lieutenant and less than two months to become a captain. Yet John Rodney never turned to piracy; he just lingered as an ineffectual captain for another sixty years.

The Black Book used by Bartholomew Grace really did exist. It contained the old Laws of Oleron as introduced to England in the twelfth century by King Richard I. A museum piece when it was last seen around 1800, the Black Book disappeared from the High Court of the Admiralty just in time to appear aboard Grace's little *Prudence*.

There are many, many books about pirates and buccaneers. One of the first ever written, dating to 1724 and often credited to Daniel Defoe, can still be bought in new editions with the title *A General History of the Pyrates*. Two of my more modern favourites are *Pirates*, by David Mitchell, and especially the wonderful *Under the Black Flag*, by David Cordingly, who reveals the sometimes disappointing truth behind the legendary buccaneers.

Acknowledgements

This last adventure of John Spencer began in a newspaper office in a little city on the northwest coast of Canada. The office belonged to Bruce Wishart, the publisher and editor of Prince Rupert's weekly paper, and we talked for hours about pirates and schooners and cannons.

A short haul up the hill was the Prince Rupert Library, where the story came into shape to fit the facts unearthed by research librarian Kathleen Larkin. The realities of tropical fever sent the *Dragon* to a place of swamps and mud. The real-life search for Captain Kidd's treasure took her to Culebra and brought Dasher in his brig. The picture that the word *Caribbean* might have raised in an Englishman's mind in 1802 gave John a fear of cannibals and gave Roland Abbey an eagerness to get a shot at his picaroons.

My father took as much interest in this last adventure as he did in the first, tracking down books about pirates and ships. He read the first draft, as he did with *The Wreckers* and *The Smugglers*, finding my mistakes and inconsistencies and embarrassing gaffes with a thoroughness that he called nitpicking but I called invaluable.

Jane Jordan Browne, my agent, suggested improvements

that sent the story in new and exciting directions.

Lauri Hornik was my editor at Random House when I began the story. She helped it through its early stages, but when she moved to a different publisher the project was passed on to Françoise Bui, who found failings in the book that no one else had seen. It's due to her that Horn appears in his lifeboat a thousand miles from land. She improved the stories in many ways.

Through it all, my wife, Kristin Miller, put up with a houseful of books, with martial music and "Heart of Oak", and even with the sound of cannons as I staged my little battles on a computer screen.

To all these people I owe my thanks and great appreciation. I am lucky to know them.

About the Author

Iain Lawrence learned to sail at the age of nine on a tiny lake on the prairies and has been an avid sailor ever since. He has owned a variety of boats, from a navy whaler to a dinghy that he built out of paper just to see if it would float. He now sails a wooden cutter called *Connection*.

With his longtime partner, Kristin Miller, and their little dog, the Skipper, Iain Lawrence makes lengthy voyages up and down the northwest coast, from Puget Sound to Alaska, exploring the far-flung islets and inlets of British Columbia. He has written two nonfiction books about his experiences.

A former journalist, he writes full-time. His two critically acclaimed companions to *The Buccaneers* — *The Wreckers* (an Edgar Allan Poe Award nominee) and *The Smugglers* — were both published by Delacorte Press.

Iain Lawrence makes his home in the Gulf Islands of British Columbia.

Sail with John Spencer on his
exciting voyages in the
HIGH SEAS ADVENTURES

The Wreckers

By Iain Lawrence

England 1799. John Spencer is fourteen when his
father's ship, the *Isle of Skye*, is shipwrecked on
Cornwall's treacherous rocky coast, guided by the
lights from a cliff-top village. John fears he is the only
survivor of the disaster, and soon learns to his horror
that the villagers are wreckers — pirates who lure
ships ashore to plunder their cargo... When John
discovers that his father also survived but is being
held prisoner by the villagers, he is determined to
rescue him — but who can he trust to help?

An imprint of HarperCollins*Publishers*

Sail with John Spencer on his
exciting voyages in the
HIGH SEAS ADVENTURES

The Smugglers
By Iain Lawrence

John Spencer is now sixteen. He's too charmed
by the pretty Dragon to heed the warning that
she was once a smugglers' vessel, as he prepares
for a trip to Dover. But soon John is forced to
consider the ominous signs. Could a ship that's
seen a smuggling run truly be spoiled for
anything else? And what does John really
know about his "bonny" crew of four?

An imprint of HarperCollins*Publishers*

Lord of the Nutcracker Men

BY IAIN LAWRENCE

It's 1914 and Johnny's father has gone to war, to the mud and trenches of France. He has made Johnny an army of toy soldiers, and Johnny fights hard with them, like a real soldier, like his dad.

But soon, the letters that arrive from France tell the ugly truth – and the new soldiers Johnny's father carves and encloses begin to show the strain. For the first time Johnny is afraid. When he fights his battles out in the garden, could he be controlling his father's fate, and even the outcome of the war itself?

An imprint of HarperCollins*Publishers*